Praise for
THE BAILEY GAME

'A powerful and thought-provoking book. Highly
recommended.'
In Print

'A well-written, sensitive exploration of a theme
central to the lives of most children.'
Independent on Sunday

'This chilling evocation of the world of a tough
junior school has conscience and cowardice
fighting it out in the heroine's sensitive spirit.'
Times Educational Supplement

'A volatile mixture . . . skilfully worked up into a
frenzied climax. The writing is powerful and the
convolutions of the plotlines are tightly
controlled.'
Junior Bookshelf

'Rees treats this subject brilliantly.'
Viewpoint

THE BAILEY GAME

Celia Rees lives in Warwickshire with her husband and daughter. She taught English for seventeen years, and now divides her time between writing, talking to readers in schools and libraries, and teaching creative writing at the University of Warwick Open Studies programme.

She writes for older children and teenagers and her books have wide popular appeal, combining compelling storytelling with powerful themes and subject matter. Her book *Truth or Dare* won the Stockport Children's Book Award, was shortlisted for the Angus Children's Book Award, the Portsmouth Children's Book Award and was commended for the Sheffield Children's Book Award – all of which were voted for by children. *Truth or Dare* was also shortlisted for the NASEN Special Needs Children's Book Award. Her other bestseller, *Witch Child*, was shortlisted for the Guardian Children's Fiction Award.

THE BAILEY
GAME

Celia Rees

MACMILLAN
CHILDREN'S BOOKS

First published 1994 by Macmillan Children's Books
a division of Macmillan Publishers Limited

This edition produced 2002 for
The Book People Ltd, Hall Wood Avenue,
Haydock, St Helens WA11 9UL

Associated companies throughout the world

ISBN 0 330 39830 X

3 5 7 9 8 6 4 2

A CIP catalogue record for this book is available from
the British Library.

Typeset by Intype London Ltd
Printed and bound in Great Britain by Mackays of Chatham plc, Kent

For Mary

Acknowledgements

I would like to thank members of BTEC Media 2, 1992–3, Henley College, Coventry, for their help and advice; the charity, KIDSCAPE; and my editor, Susan Houlden.

Chapter 1

'Did you see that?'

Josie Campbell's question brought Alex back to the lunch-time playground with an uncomfortable lurch.

'What? See what?'

Josie looked up sharply, puzzled by the other girl's sudden intensity.

'What's the matter, Alex? You look like you've seen a ghost or something.'

Alexandra Lewis did not believe in ghosts, she had to have real proof before she believed in anything but, just for a second, she thought she saw him, standing on his own, quite still, amid the roaring chaos of the school yard. Michael Bailey. He was wearing his shiny blue snorkel parka with the fur-fringed hood up so it shadowed his face. All you could see was his high white forehead, streaked by strands of bright ginger hair. Gritty dust patched each knee of his grey trousers and his black shoes gleamed dull in the bright April sun. Then, in the time it takes to blink and frown, he'd gone.

If Josie had seen him too . . .

But she hadn't. She was pointing in the opposite direction, pulling on Alex's sleeve now, trying to focus her attention.

'Over there! Look! Sandi Mitchell. She's chatting up Greg Simpson!'

1

Was that all? Alex fell back against the wall in relief.

'So what?' she said, glancing over at the centre of the playground.

Sandi was standing right in the middle of a football game. She had threaded her way through and cut Greg out of the play with more skill than the opposing centre forward. He held the ball now, spinning it on his fingers, sending it up into the air, as he listened to Sandi. Neither of them took the slightest notice of the other players, standing around in helpless frustration.

'She's asking him out!' Josie's voice squeaked high with excitement.

'Why shouldn't she?' Alex shrugged. 'It's a free country.'

'But she's supposed to be going out with David Morris!' Josie giggled with delight. 'Look at him. Over there in goal. He's seen them – he's going all red!' She tightened her grip on Alex's arm and hopped up and down in excitement. 'Perhaps there'll be a fight! You'll be all right. He's free to go out with you now, Alex. I'll ask him if you like.'

David Morris stood for a moment, blushing and indecisive, and then walked away, tearing off his goalkeeping gloves and throwing them down onto the pile of coats that marked the posts.

'If you say anything to him,' Alex hissed at Josie, 'I'll personally kill you. You got that?'

Josie's brows contracted in hurt offence. 'I thought you liked David. I thought you wanted to go out with him. You said you fancied him.'

'I didn't exactly say that,' Alex replied, trying to control her temper.

'Yes, you did. You told me last week when we went to the park. I remember because . . .'

Alex remembered the conversation. She'd had to say something to shut Josie up, to stop her going on and on. She didn't like talking about boys like that, especially David, it made her feel uncomfortable.

'Like I said,' she folded her arms, glaring down at the other girl, 'one word and you're dead.'

'OK, OK,' Josie backed away. 'I'm going over to Sandi, anyhow. See what's happening.'

Sandi Mitchell had rejoined a group on the opposite side of the playground. Most of the girls in Alex's class quickly clustered round her. Andrea Bowman was stuffing her skipping rope back in her bag, something more interesting had come up. Boys. At the moment it seemed the only thing any of them wanted to talk about.

Alex stayed where she was. She had no desire to join in. Suddenly it had become impossible to just be friends with a boy, like she was with David. Even a smile in his direction was enough to start a whisper that she wanted to go out with him. They were being so stupid about it. Going out with somebody didn't mean what they thought it did. Helen, Alex's older sister, was fifteen and pretty secretive about what she and her friends did when they went out with boys, but Alex suspected it involved more than hanging around watching them play football, or trying to get them to play kiss chase.

She looked away from Sandi and her little group of admirers, back towards the space where, for that strange second, she thought she'd seen Michael Bailey. Was it a ghost? No. She couldn't accept that.

3

There could be, there had to be, another explanation. An idea, any idea could pop into your head, right? So why not a person? Perhaps that's what ghosts were. Ideas of people that just came, appearing and disappearing, for no reason. That must be it. That made sense. Alex shook her head and grinned. Her imagination really had her going back there, just for a minute.

She braced one foot against the wall and folded her arms. For a lot of the people running around in front of her, Michael Bailey was a ghost, and a real one. He was as real to them as these bricks or Alex herself. They could tell you all about him. What he ate, what he did. They could even take you and show you where he lived.

He lived in the caretaker's garage. Alex could see the top squares of its smeared dusty windows peering over the wall at her like a pair of bleary eyes. One of the doors was rotted at the corner, the paint had peeled back and the wood showed like brown crumbling teeth. It looked like a giant rat's hole. That's how Bailey gets in and out, they whispered to each other. He comes out after dark most nights, and if there's a full moon, always. He looks for food; if he finds any living creature, he drains all its blood. Otherwise he searches about for left-overs, sucking out the flat dregs from drink cans, feeding himself on half-eaten bags of crisps, sandwich crusts, squashed biscuits. That's how the Bailey stories went. Now only the bravest would go anywhere near the garage and only the bravest of the brave would stand on shaking tiptoe to look in.

All it contained was broken desks and chairs that

the caretaker was supposed to repair. Alex knew that for an absolute fact. All the stories were so much bull, but still they went round and round. Anything that disappeared, anything that couldn't be found, Bailey had taken it. Some of the Infants had even started leaving scraps of food by the bike sheds, as near as they dared to the garage door, hoping if they did that he wouldn't come looking for more.

The older ones said they didn't believe it but they didn't come up there out of school-time, to play football or mess around in the yard. Even on Parents' Nights, if dusk was falling, the playground was deserted.

There were other stories, too, about what had happened to Bailey. Some were comic in a sick sort of way, most of them were as gory as a horror story. Alex walked away when people talked about it because it was stupid. Ridiculous. Half of them hadn't been at the school when it happened. They didn't even know he was dead. Not for sure.

Alex shivered despite the warm spring sun with its promise of summer to come, and moved to a nearby bench. She didn't want to think about Bailey any more. Her attention shifted to Sandi Mitchell.

Sandi twiddled with her fancy pink polka-dot sunglasses and smiled at the huddle of girls giggling and shrieking around her, all eager to know about her latest conquest, desperate for every little detail. She handed the sunglasses to Andrea and re-adjusted the slides in her long fair hair, getting ready to move on to herself and how attractive she was – her other favourite topic.

I am the most conceited person in the entire universe, Alex mouthed, copying Sandi's self-satisfied smirk, and I'm so lucky, even with this hair I tan so easily. She began miming Sandi, tossing her own thick, tangled, curly brown hair, smoothing her T-shirt, pulling her shorts up to get more sun. She heard a low laugh from the other end of the bench and stopped in mid action.

Alex was sharing the seat with Lauren Price. The other girl's grey eyes met hers in mocking laughter. Alex had never even seen her smile before, Lauren generally scowled at the world from under her long black fringe and thick drawn together eyebrows. An extra-large T-shirt, splashed with some fluorescent surfing message, bagged over faded jeans ripped at the knees. Her thin brown arms were folded tightly across her chest, her long fingers disappearing up huge sleeves which drooped past her elbows.

Lauren was new to the school. Her parents had recently moved from Australia. This had caused quite a sensation at first, but interest soon faded when people found out she'd never lived anywhere near Ramsey Street. They had been told to be nice to her, and of course they were, when teachers were around. It was different in the playground. Everyone ignored her. If you were new, it could take weeks, months, before you were accepted. Some people never were. Alex grinned back a second too late and the smile died in Lauren's eyes. The other girl's hands had balled into fists again and she thrust them deep in her pockets, sprawling her long legs out. A little kid, running past ringing the bell for the end of lunch-time, had to swerve to avoid being tripped up.

Alex got up to go and glanced briefly over at Lauren, but she was looking away now, pointedly staring in the opposite direction.

The noisy, jostling groups thinned to ones and twos and then solitary individuals, but Lauren stayed where she was. She hated getting ready to go into class. She delayed joining the rest of them until the last possible minute. Lining up, with them all chattering excitedly to each other, just made her feel more alone. The fact that nobody spoke to her made her feel even less accepted.

Mrs Bridges, the Deputy Head, waited impatiently for the class to assemble. She was tapping her pen on the dog-eared register, and complaining about them to Ms Quaid, the temporary teacher. Ms Quaid looked more like a student than a regular member of staff because she was young and had one long thin beaded plait in her short red hair. She wore mini-skirts and Doc Martens. Red lipstick and dangly earrings also marked her as different and in the classroom she smiled a lot, sometimes she even laughed out loud; not like Mrs Dunbar, their proper teacher, who'd left to have a baby.

Ms Quaid wasn't laughing now, though, Alex noticed. She was looking serious and listening as Bridges told her what an awful class they were. The Deputy Head looked down her long thin nose as she spoke, and prodded at particular examples within her reach with the business end of her Biro.

'. . . wouldn't believe they were the top class,' she was saying as Alex came up. 'Just look at them! Disgrace to the school. Can't trust them an inch. Won't be sorry to see this lot go, I can tell you . . .'

7

Josie stayed with Sandi and her friends. She turned her back when Alex joined the line, and made no attempt to join her.

Alex shrugged with resignation. Josie wasn't really her friend, anyway. She didn't even particularly like her. She had just been there, that's all, at the beginning of term after Lisa moved away for good at Easter. Alex and Lisa had been best friends for years, all the way up the school. Neither of them had believed Lisa would really go, her family had been discussing it for ever. They wouldn't be able to sell their house and even if they did, they wouldn't find a new one. Her mum would refuse to leave, or her dad would hate his new job and it would all be called off.

But that had not happened. The day had finally come around and the last thing Alex saw was Lisa's tear-streaked face peering through a gap between a squashed-up duvet and a box of Pampers. Then the car was gone and she'd been left, waving at an empty street. How could they stay friends like before, with Lisa hundreds of miles away now, up in Newcastle?

The doors opened and 7Q surged forward. Alex walked in with Lauren Price but although they were jostled and pushed and surrounded by noise, they were careful to keep a space between them and neither said anything to the other.

Chapter 2

'Alexandra Lewis.'

'Present, Ms Quaid.' Alex answered afternoon registration in the same automatic singsong as everyone else.

'Sandra Mitchell.'

Nothing. Silence stretched out. Ms Quaid repeated the name and glanced up to meet a snuffle of suppressed giggles.

'Sandra Mitchell, will you please respond when your name is called?'

Still no answer.

Ms Quaid looked up again and the giggles grew louder.

'Sandra, answer! You are obviously here. I'm staring right at you.'

Sandi studied her fingernails and then looked round at her friends.

'I told you before it's not my name, Miss. So I'm not going to answer to it. My name's Sandi now. Sandi with an "i". I want it altered in the register 'cos I'm having it changed by deed poll.'

Ms Quaid sighed heavily and turned her eyes up to the ceiling. As she picked up her pen, Sandi spoke again.

'While you're at it, you can change my middle name to Yolande.' The giggles were spreading out now. Sandi grinned, sensing the class's appreciation, announcing, 'Sandi Yolande Mitchell. That's me.'

'This is a legal document, Sandra. I can't go monkeying about with it. Sandra Brenda Joyce Mitchell,' Ms Quaid read out. 'That's who you are and that's who you'll stay.'

All over the room, different voices howled out the unfamiliar names gleefully. Sandi turned, scowling, red-faced and furious, into the swelling laughter. Ms Quaid grinned at Sandi, describing a '1' in the air, before carrying on to the end of the register.

Sandi's continued glaring subdued most of the laughter, but there was still a ripple of amusement and the odd muttering of the names, even when Ms Quaid was sorting out the materials for the afternoon's lesson.

'What do you think you're laughing at?'

Sandi's outburst could have been directed at anyone but she was looking at Lauren Price.

'Your name, of course,' the Australian girl's voice drawled back at her across the classroom. She paused for a moment, as if to consider. 'Brenda Joyce – suits you.'

The laughter burst out again and Sandi stood up.

'What about your name?' she screamed across the classroom. 'Your name is really stupid. You've got a name no one's ever heard of!'

'I have,' Ms Quaid said coolly. 'Lauren Bacall, right?' Lauren nodded, blushing slightly. 'Now, sit down, Sandi – and shut up. What's the matter with you? Can't you take a joke?'

No, she couldn't. All that afternoon, as they were working on different assignments for their conservation project, Sandi seethed. Alex felt the atmosphere in the classroom change. There was a tingle of tension and excitement, it was being charged up with a certain sort of energy, like a battery.

She glanced round the room. Greg Simpson was over on Sandi's table now. Ms Quaid had given him permission to stay there for the afternoon. She wasn't the pushover Dunbar was but unless Greg was actively doing something wrong, she didn't go out of her way to antagonize him. But he was quiet, they all seemed to be working, heads together. That might fool Quaid, Alex thought, but it doesn't fool me. There was something about the way they kept giggling and popping their heads up to look about before ducking down again. They were up to something.

Alex disliked Greg. She didn't think she was scared of him, but she avoided having to put that to the test by making sure she never had much to do with him. He had a gang: the Bridge Boys. They reckoned they were hard but they weren't as hard as the original Bridge Boys, led by Del, Greg's older brother. Greg wasn't as bad as Del either, yet, but he was working on it.

He was one of the tallest in the class and powerfully built and he would not hesitate to use his advantage over the rest to frighten and intimidate. He wore his brown hair long at the moment, parted high on his head, almost in the middle, and was constantly flicking it back out of his eyes to show how shiny it was. He wore an earring in one ear and, in his own way, he was as vain as Sandi. Something about his eyes and his narrow grinning mouth reminded Alex of an Alsatian dog, but she was careful not to share this observation.

He was talking intensely to Andrea Bowman at that moment, jabbing and pointing, giving her some kind of instructions. She was nodding obediently, concentrating on what he was saying, so Alex could watch them without being noticed.

Andrea was Sandi's best friend. She tried to copy Sandi in everything, she'd even shortened her name to Andi with an 'i', but so far no one had taken it up. She tried to wear the same clothes but they never looked right on her and her hair was always escaping from the Sandi-style slides she'd started wearing. A huge pair of blue-rimmed glasses dwarfed Andrea's face and she seemed to have more teeth than most people. The braces she'd recently had fitted showed like a badge on each tooth as she grinned at Greg Simpson. She worshipped Sandi, but Alex had the idea that she was an accessory, there to make Sandi herself look good, and that the feeling was not exactly mutual.

Andrea got up and Alex quickly went back to her work, before they noticed her staring. She sat doodling on the desk trying to think of ways to make her report about their recent trip to a plastic recycling unit more interesting, but she couldn't concentrate. The atmosphere in the classroom reminded her of something.

Then she realized what it was. She gripped her pen so tightly the point bit into the worn surface of the desk, etching a jagged blue scar across the rest of the graffiti. For a moment she didn't dare look up, but continued to stare at the mark she'd just made in the desk top, in case he was there again, like in the playground, and this time her glance might actually meet the sad slaty-blue eyes of Michael Bailey. It would be as if they were all back in Mrs Harris's class, still playing the Game and thinking of ways to get Michael Bailey.

Towards the end of the afternoon, Sandi let out a loud indignant cry that silenced the room.

'Miss! Miss! My sunglasses. They aren't here! They've disappeared!'

Ms Quaid stood up from where she'd been bending over helping someone with their work.

'What's the matter, Sandi? What's happened?'

She held her hands up eventually, cutting Sandi short. The account was getting as long and detailed as a police report. She glanced round, frowning. A good search would take ages and the bell was about to go. She quickly made her decision. It wasn't difficult. The classroom was in a real mess and she wasn't feeling that well disposed towards Sandi Mitchell after her performance at registration.

'I'm sure they'll turn up somewhere, Sandi,' she said briskly. 'Everyone can have a really good look when they tidy up, can't they? Hear that, people? Be on the lookout for Sandi's sunglasses. Time to clear up now.'

'But, Miss . . .' Sandi protested – this was not the reaction she had expected. 'Someone might have taken them, they might have hidden them. I think you should . . .'

'Should what, Sandi?' Ms Quaid's voice took on a

13

harder edge. 'Are you telling me how to do my job?'

'No, Miss. But someone might have stolen them . . .'

'Are you accusing anybody?'

Sandi looked at Andrea and Greg. Andrea nodded to go on, but Greg replied with a slight shake of the head.

'No, not exactly. But Mrs Dunbar always . . .'

Always kept them for hours and practically strip-searched them, Alex thought.

'It may have escaped your notice, Sandra' – the young teacher's voice was icy now – 'but I am not Mrs Dunbar. You have been told not to bring items of value to school often enough. If you misplace them, it's your own lookout.'

She turned away from the trio, not prepared to discuss it further. Alex watched them. They were sulking now, eyeing the teacher balefully. Somehow, without knowing it, Quaid had completely ruined some kind of plan. They took no part in the tidy-up and slipped out as soon as the bell went, muttering angrily.

Chapter 3

Alex had stayed behind to help clear up and now she was late. She was out of the cloakroom in record time. She didn't want to stay on her own in there any longer than she had to. That place, with its scatter of left-behind coats and faintly swinging pump bags, and the distant drip of taps and seeping smell from the boys' toilets, reminded her too much of Michael Bailey.

The last time she'd seen him, in real life, the last time he'd been at school, had been two years ago. It had been cold. Cold for the time of year. Mrs Harris, their teacher then, had turned the heating up and made some crack about spring never coming. Some people had got excited, thinking it was going to snow, as they'd stared out at the driving sleet on that freezing afternoon.

The next day, the day after it happened, in Assembly, the silence had gone on and on until they knew: even the Headmaster didn't know what to say, or what to do. It had been the old Head then, Mr Jenkins. He had smoothed back his few thin strands of grey hair and cleared his throat a couple of times before he started. And then, to Alex's complete amazement, he'd gone on about a schoolboy prank. A stupid schoolboy prank that could so easily have turned into a tragic accident, that's how he'd described it.

Alex had stared at the pock-marked wooden floor between her knees, unable to look at him. 'Schoolboy prank' and Michael Bailey did not go together. Didn't he know that? How could it have been an accident? Everyone sitting in front of him knew it was the last part of a Game. The Bailey Game.

She had hardly listened as he had gone on to tell them they were not to blame, it was not their fault, not to feel badly about it. No one did anything more. That had been the finish. Mr Jenkins retired the year after and, to Alex's knowledge, he never again spoke about it.

Alex hurried to catch up with the last knots of kids leaving school. She suddenly wanted to be with other people and to keep out in the open; away from hidden places and shadowy corners, behind the temporary classrooms, around the back of the sheds. Places that you can find if you want to, if you don't want people to see you, if you need somewhere private. That had been important in the Bailey Game – privacy and being secret.

She went towards the cycleway footbridge that goes over the bypass and watched the last few groups and stragglers make their way across. It was her clear route home but that particular evening she took another. It was miles out of her way, it would take her twice as long, but she just could not make herself cross that place.

She was careful not to step on any cracks in the pavement and to touch every tree. She counted the lampposts and chanted the colours of the cars that passed, just like she did when Helen was six and

16

she was three, anything to stop her thinking about Michael Bailey.

It didn't work. He kept coming back.

What was it about him that had made them hate him so much? Had he really been that different from other kids? It had seemed so then, he'd seemed like a freak, a monster. But thinking back, he seemed just – ordinary. He was a bit of a loner, but he hadn't had much choice, it wasn't clear that he was naturally like that. He wasn't especially good at anything, but neither was he especially bad. Maybe it was his name, or his plumpish build, or his red hair and high forehead, or his clothes, or the way he wore his bag slung across his chest, maybe it was things as trivial as that. There was nothing you could point to in particular, but somehow all of them together had marked him out as the butt of all their jokes and what had started as mocking and ridicule had ended in vicious hatred.

Alex entered the new estate where she lived. The road twisted and turned through the houses. Each house had its own separate space and they were dotted about at odd angles to make them appear different from each other. The houses were quite big inside but from the outside they were designed to look small and quaint. The whole place resembled a toy model village more than a modern housing estate. Alex preferred the house they had lived in before, even though it had no garden to speak of and was so small they were all constantly on top of each other, but nobody else did and when they moved she hadn't been consulted.

She walked up the path by the side of the dinky little lawn and peered through the glass door before she inserted her key. Helen was home. She could see all her stuff strewn up the hall. That was one good thing about this house, they didn't have to share a bedroom. Alex was neat and liked to keep everything tidy, Helen was messy to the point of obsessiveness. Alex pushed the door against Helen's bag, which she'd dropped just inside the hall, and squeezed in.

'Alex? Is that you?' Her mother's voice came down the passage from the kitchen.

'No, it's a mad axeman come to murder both of you,' Alex muttered to herself before shouting, 'Yes, it's me.'

'Do you want a cup of tea?' her mother called back. 'We're down in the kitchen.'

Alex picked up Helen's blazer and then her cardigan. Helen discarded clothing like some creatures shed their shells, things just lay where they fell. Alex listened for a moment as she draped them neatly over the bannister. Helen's voice was droning on, punctuated by Mum saying 'nhnh' and 'that's nice, dear'. Alex decided not to go in. She'd been trapped like that before. Mum would ask what sort of day she'd had and as soon as she started to say, Helen would interrupt and then they'd both completely ignore her.

'I'm going up to my room, Mum,' she shouted from the foot of the stairs. 'I've got homework to do.'

'Righto,' her mother's voice drifted up the stairs after her. 'I'll call you when tea's ready.'

Alex sat down at her desk and got out her half-written article on the plastic re-cycling plant. The doodles in the margin acted as another reminder and now, in the secure familiarity of her well-ordered room, she stopped fighting the memory.

Jack, their young tabby cat, jumped up, purring and nudging at her hand. She fondled his ears absently and he began to push harder with his bullety head, demanding more attention.

'Get off, Jack,' Alex muttered and shoved him roughly off her knee.

He fell in an ungainly heap at her feet and looked up at her, hurt and puzzled, but she took no notice. He finally stalked off on his stiff little legs, swishing his thin stripy tail to show how offended he was at such unaccustomed treatment, but his displeasure was lost on Alex. She was far away. Her mind had taken her back to an entirely different time and place.

It was two years ago and she was shivering in the icy wind of a cold March morning, standing outside Year Five's temporary classroom, waiting to go in.

Chapter 4

'Here he is. Here he is.'

Sandra Mitchell nudged Alex Lewis excitedly. They were watching out for Mrs Harris and waiting for Michael Bailey. He did not look at them as he approached, just studied the asphalt beneath his feet.

'Phew, what's that smell?' Sandra said loudly, wrinkling her nose. Then whispered to Alex, 'You start.'

'Hey, Bailey!' Alex shouted, but he still would not look at them. 'Where'd you get those clothes from? Round A Pound or Oxfam?'

'No,' interrupted Josie, 'they're out of his mum's rag-bag. Aren't they, Bailey?'

'No, they aren't.' Sandra picked up the speculation. 'They're off some tramp's washing line.'

'Love the coat, Bailey.' Alex Lewis faked an admiring stare as Bailey skirted round her. 'Must tell me where you got it. I want to get one just like it.'

The three girls' shrieking laughter followed him into the classroom. Michael Bailey made his way to his desk through the usual chorus of comments and shouts. Some of them waved hands in front of their noses as he passed, as if a bad smell had come into the classroom.

There was even a rhyme about him. It started now in his head.

Bailey's smelly, Bailey's smelly,
sleeps in a skip,
smells of . . .

That was just the beginning of it. After that it got
worse, continuing on verse after verse. Some of it was
about his family, and some of it he didn't understand
really, but all of it was insulting. All of it. Sometimes
they competed with each other, seeing who could think
of the most disgusting verse. It was obscene, unprint-
able. No one was singing it that day but he never seemed
to be free from it, he even heard it in his dreams.

Michael sat on his own at the front, in the corner.
He put his bag under his desk and inspected his
chair carefully before he sat down. He opened
his desk cautiously, as though it might be rigged or
booby-trapped, and peered in. As he closed the lid
his face did not register whatever unspeakable mess
they'd put in there, but the deep-throated braying
laugh of the boys at the back did.

'What is it? What is it?' Sandra asked.

David Morris whispered something to her, and
disgust and delight flitted across her features.

'Who did it?' she said, eyes wide in admiration.

David nodded towards Greg Simpson who rocked
back on his chair, arms folded, grinning acceptance
of her appreciation.

Sandra told Alex who then told Lisa and Josie and
the news spread on round the class. Michael Bailey
sat motionless, impassive, staring away from them
out of the window. A faint blush on the back of his
neck was the only thing to show he was at all con-
scious of their intense attention.

Every time he thought he'd reached the bottom of

this pit of misery, it deepened. Every day it got worse.

The thin cold rain was turning to sleet and the weedy trees outside the window looked like they had done all winter, no sign of buds, let alone leaves. It had been so cold this morning that his mum had made him wear the new parka she'd bought him. His mouth twisted in a slight, bitter smile as he remembered her coming home with it, proud of her purchase, how she'd made him try it on, saying, 'There you are. You can be just like the other boys.'

He only turned round to face the classroom when he knew that Mrs Harris was at her desk and starting to call the register.

When she finished, she pulled her cardigan more tightly round her.

'Look at that,' she said, 'I do believe it's trying to snow. Doesn't look like spring is ever coming.'

At the mention of snow they all rushed to the window, but they were careful to avoid crowding into the area where he was sitting, none of them would ever come near him. If any one of them touched him, even accidentally, their faces contorted in horror. They would then turn and daub the next person, saying, 'Pass it on, it's the Bailey germ.'

Sometimes they would come and touch him deliberately and shriek off, chasing each other. Then it was part of a Game. 'Bailey Bacteria.'

'Come along.' Mrs Harris's voice was calling them back. 'Time for Assembly.'

They lined up in twos by the door, except for Bailey who was always at the back on his own.

'Come on, Michael.' Mrs Harris chivvied him along. 'Do stop dawdling. Catch up with the others or you'll be late.'

She watched him continue along the corridor at his usual measured pace, well behind the rest of the class. That boy was a worry, but what could you do? You couldn't make them like him, you couldn't make him popular. And once something like this started it was so hard to eradicate. They'd had the ring-leaders in, that Del Simpson was one of them – nasty little piece of work he was – and Greg, he was getting nearly as bad, but it was like squeezing a balloon, you clamped down in one place, it just popped up somewhere else. They had thought of putting him in another class, but as she'd pointed out to the Head, it would do no good. Most of it went on in the playground or out of school. They couldn't keep an eye on him twenty-four hours a day.

Michael Bailey was always last into Assembly. He worked it that way because then he'd be on the end, and the cordon of space that always existed around him would not be so obvious.

Alex Lewis moved up automatically as soon as he sat down. It had not always been like that. He looked down to the restless row of little ones at the front. Mrs McDonald, their teacher, was watching them like a hawk, fingers like talons, itching to grip the shoulders of talkers and fidgeters. He remembered when they had been in her class. She'd taken them on a nature walk one hot summer day. They had all marched in a crocodile behind her, Alex Lewis had been his partner. They had walked along chatting and laughing, just like the rest of them. He'd explained to her the difference between a swift and a swallow, showing her the little nests under the eaves of the houses. He'd even held her hand.

Chapter 5

'Alex. Alex!'

Alex came back with a start. Helen's hand was shaking her by the shoulder. She raised her head off the desk, confused, and looked around.

Helen grinned. 'Mum says to come down now, tea's ready. You were fast asleep. I'll tell her you need an early night.'

'I wasn't asleep . . .' Alex started to say.

Helen's grin faded.

'Hey,' she said, 'turn round. Into the light. Have you been crying?' She took Alex's chin in her hand. 'You have, haven't you? What's the matter?'

'Nothing. I haven't been crying.' Alex wrenched her head away and wiped her face with her sleeve. 'I'll be down in a minute. Go away and leave me alone.'

Helen's greeny-grey eyes stared down at her for a moment with a mixture of amusement and concern. Then she shrugged.

'OK, please yourself. But I'd wash your face if I was you. It's all puffy – and tears leave clean streaks, Mum'll know in a minute.'

Alex didn't talk much during dinner, but no one seemed to notice. Helen talked enough for both of them. As she talked she swept her long hair back in a way that Alex found particularly irritating. When Helen did it, her straight, tawny hair stayed in place. If Alex tried it, her short curly hair just stuck up and made her look like Ed the Duck.

'Next time I go to the hairdresser's,' Helen was saying to her mother, 'I'm going to have highlights, what do you think?'

'No, you're not,' their father said without looking up. 'I'm not having a daughter of mine going round with bleached hair looking like a floozie. Tell her, Janet.'

'Dad! You don't know anything about it. Tell him, Mum.'

Mum looked from one to the other. Lately Helen and Dad had been having one argument after another. Alex couldn't stand the wrangling and didn't like watching her mother having to act as piggy in the middle. She decided to go upstairs before she got dragged into it.

'I'm going to finish my homework.'

Her mother regarded her critically. 'You haven't eaten very much. Don't you want some pudding?'

'No, thanks. I'm not hungry.'

'I'll have hers, then,' Helen said as she put down her knife and fork.

'You've been very quiet,' her mum said, as Alex got up from the table.

'Probably sickening for something.' Helen helped herself to apple crumble. 'When I went to get her she was sound asleep, head on the table.'

'I was not!' Alex answered angrily. 'I was just thinking about something.'

'You weren't, you were fast asleep,' Helen countered, 'snoring like a little pig. I tell you, Mum, she's definitely sickening for something.'

'Do you feel all right?'

Alex shot her sister a thanks-a-lot look as her mum felt her forehead.

'I'm fine, Mum. Honestly. I'm just not very hungry.'

'She ought to have an early night,' Helen added through a mouthful of crumble.

She left them talking about what could be wrong with her as if she was about four or some special case, not part of the family. She really hated them when they did that. Especially Helen, who seemed to think that being fifteen qualified her to join in.

When she had finished her homework, she had a bath and washed her hair. She stayed in the water until it was cool and all Helen's Body Shop bubble stuff had dispersed into grey scum. When she left the bathroom the house was quiet. Her family were in the lounge, faint television laughter filtered up the stairs. Alex sighed and went up to her room. She didn't really want to be alone, but neither did she want to join them.

Alex towelled her hair, her mind drifting back to Michael Bailey. They really had made his life unbearable. They all had, she'd been as bad, she'd joined in. It made her sad to think about it now, and terribly ashamed. It had made her cry, whatever she had said to Helen. But back then she'd been the same as everybody else. She had really believed the chants and insults. He was a slap-head, stupid and fat, smelly and ugly. The thought of his touch had been enough to make her shiver with loathing.

She remembered one day, a Saturday, and not long before it happened. She'd seen him with his mum in the library. He'd been at the counter holding a pile of books and, as he put them down, his mother had smiled affectionately, saying something to the librarian and he'd laughed shyly, his pale skin flushing with pleasure. Alex had watched from behind a length of shelves, her own face burning with shame, realizing he was just like her, just like anybody.

She picked up her brush and went over to the mirror. That was two years ago. She looked at her reflection carefully before she started to brush out her hair. She'd changed, they all had, two years made a big difference. She went quickly to her desk, found that year's class photograph and propped it up next to the mirror. Mrs Harris looked the same but everyone else had changed. She hadn't seen this one for ages and studied it for a moment, shocked at how young they all looked. She scrutinized her own image on the photograph and compared it with the one she saw in the mirror. She was much taller and her face less rounded, her hazel eyes looked larger. Her hair was still curly and the same light brown but now it was cut in a proper style.

She checked the others, scanning the rows. There was David, she smiled slightly, ears sticking out and his mouth half open, like he was about to say something. And Greg in the row at the back, hair cropped short, arms folded, his dark eyes squinting into the camera. Sandi was in the next row down, hair in a pony-tail, and Andrea at the front, kneeling on the

27

floor, wearing a snaggle-toothed grin and round plastic glasses stuck together with sticking plaster.

Bailey wasn't on it, of course, it had been taken in the summer. They'd all changed since then, on the outside at least. Surely what happened to him, what they had done to him, meant it could never happen to anyone again, didn't it?

So why this feeling she'd had, in class that afternoon? It had been strong. Powerful enough to take her back two years, to get old photos out, to take her back to a time she had tried to put out of her mind, a time she tried to blank out.

She put the class photograph face down and sat on her bed, staring into space. What did it mean? Was it going to start all over again? And who would it be this time? Who was the next Michael Bailey?

Chapter 6

'Alex!' Helen appeared round the door, fully dressed. 'Mum says do you know what time it is? You better get up right now or you'll be late for school.'

'Yeah, all right. I'm coming,' Alex mumbled.

She felt more tired than when she went to bed. All night long she'd been having dreams, except they felt more like memories than dreams. She'd been back on that footbridge again and again. She could only remember rags and scraps, but the overwhelming, heart-pounding fear had left her feeling weak now and depressed.

'Come on, Alex,' her mother said as she finished her breakfast. 'I'll give you a lift to school if you hurry up and get your things ready.'

As Alex wiped her mouth and raced off to clean her teeth and get her stuff, her mood lifted slightly. It wasn't even raining and Mum didn't usually offer, even if it was bucketing down.

A couple of miles across town, Lauren Price lay on her bed, hands behind her head, staring at blue Australian sky and silver surf. She was concentrating her whole mind on getting into her Bondi Beach poster, trying to turn her mother's shouts from downstairs into the sound of seagulls calling to her.

Her bedroom door opened and Lauren shifted her gaze. Her mother was standing there with her coat on, jingling her car keys.

'Lauren, will you come on? I've been calling you for the last ten minutes!'

'I'm not going, Mum,' Lauren replied, closing her eyes. 'I'm sick.'

Her mother sighed as she came over to the bed.

'What's the matter?' she asked, feeling her daughter's forehead.

'I don't know.' Lauren shook her hand away. 'I just don't feel well. I'll have to stay home today. I've got a headache and my stomach feels funny.'

Mrs Price looked down at her daughter, trying to decide what to do. Lauren was rather pale, but there was no temperature. She seemed to have slept all right and had been fine going to bed last night. This was the third time this had happened in so many weeks and each time, as soon as nine o'clock passed, Lauren had staged a remarkable recovery.

'Come on,' she said, sitting down on the bed. 'I know you're not ill . . .'

'I am, Mum.' Lauren turned to face her. 'Honestly.'

She put her hand gently on her daughter's shoulder. 'I know something's wrong, Lauren. What is it? Is it something to do with school? Why won't you tell me?'

'No. It's nothing like that,' Lauren muttered. 'I just feel poorly.'

Somewhere downstairs a radio jingle sounded for the 8:30 news.

'It's the doctor for you, then,' her mother said as

she stood up. 'We'll drop Caroline off and then I'll take you straight round to see her.'

That should do the trick, Mrs Price thought. Ever since she was little, Lauren would rather visit the dentist any day than spend time in a doctor's surgery.

'Oh, all right.' Her daughter scowled. 'I'll go then!'

There was the usual traffic chaos outside the school, with parents trying to drop their children as near as possible to the main entrance. I hope we're really late, Lauren thought, as her mother stopped for the crossing warden to shepherd his flock of mothers, towing small children and pushing buggies, across the road. Then, as he retreated, a car moved away from the kerb. Her mother indicated left, slowed to let the driver out, and pulled in to the side of the road.

'Bye, girls. Have a good day.'

She leaned over to open the passenger door. The handle was stiff and Caroline, her younger daughter, was having trouble with it.

'Bye, Mum. And you,' Caroline said, leaning over to kiss her before scrambling out.

'Lauren!' her mother called.

Lauren leaned down and looked through the passenger door. 'What?'

'Aren't you even going to say goodbye?'

'Oh, yeah. Bye,' she said with a negligent wave and turned away, grabbing Caroline by the arm to steer her through the crowds.

Mrs Price sat for a moment watching them in her

rear-view mirror. Lauren had changed so much since they came to Britain. She was like a different girl. She'd become so quiet and withdrawn. She'd always been such a sunny one, chattering away, now she'd lost her brilliant ready smile and hardly said a word, unless it was to bite your head off.

They'd known it would be a wrench, leaving the neighbourhood and their school and all their friends but she'd never have thought Lauren would take it so hard. Caroline was the one she'd worried about. Shows you what I know, she thought, turning the ignition. Caroline had settled right in. Couldn't stop her talking about it. She had her little friends round to tea and spent entire weekends at other people's houses. She indicated to pull out. But Lauren? Nothing. She wouldn't speak about school. Mrs Price realized she did not know the name of one child in her class; in Caroline's she could name them all. Each night, when she asked how the day had gone, her enquiries were met with stony silence or monosyllables.

Guilt tugged at her as she stared in her mirror at the passing traffic. Lauren had not wanted to come here, had always hated the idea, and she had picked up at least some of that from her mother. Jenny Price hadn't wanted to leave, either. She was a native Australian, it was her country. It was different for Jeff, her husband, he was English. The rows they'd had when he'd told her about the move. But they were here now. They had to make the best of it. It would be easier when Jeff was home more. That was another thing, he'd been so busy with his job, they'd hardly seen him.

She came to with a start, realizing the car behind

had just flashed her twice. She acknowledged the gesture with an embarrassed smile and a wave and pulled out into the road.

'Who's that?' Alex's mother said as she edged into the space.

'Who's who?' Alex peered around.

'That woman, who's just pulled out in that red car.'

Alex shrugged. 'How should I know?'

'That tall girl over there, just got out. No, over there, just going in. Looks about your age. Is she in your class? Is that her sister?'

'Oh, that's Lauren Price,' Alex said. 'And yes, she's in my class and I suppose that must be her sister, unless she's into kidnapping.'

'What a striking looking girl. Funny, I never heard you mention her.'

Alex shrugged again and reached in the back for her bag. 'She's new. Come from Australia.'

'That must be it. I've known half these people for years,' Alex's mother said, pointing to a knot of women standing gossiping after having delivered their children, 'and they still don't give me the time of day. Then a total stranger smiles and waves.' She grinned. 'It's nice to know there's at least one other human parent.'

Alex leaned over to kiss her mother before getting out of the car.

'Got to go, Mum. Or we'll both be late.'

'Yes, love. See you later.'

Lauren watched Caroline run off to join her friends before reluctantly turning into the senior playground. She felt the day stretching out in front of her. She had not realized until she came here that days could be so long or that it was possible to be so miserable. Why had they come here? The anger and resentment she felt about the move had not lessened, it had grown, making her feel hard and bitter. In this place she was a stranger even to herself. She hated it here so much, the longing for her old school, and her old friends was like a physical ache inside her.

Each group from her class deliberately turned away as she passed. She had made a real effort to be nice and friendly at the start, but all she'd ever received was rejection from them, the cold shoulder. It won't be as bad as you think, her mum had said as they were packing up, but it was. It was worse, much worse. It was so bad Lauren had started to think the unthinkable. In her secret heart she wanted her mum to leave her dad and take them back to Australia.

Alex apologized for her slight lateness, gave in her homework, and settled into free-reading time.

'Hey, Alex. Alex,' Josie whispered over the top of her magazine.

'What?' Alex said, without looking up from her book.

'Thought any more about David? Sandi's dumped him for definite.'

Alex turned a page and muttered, 'What are you telling me for? I told you yesterday. Not interested.'

'I don't believe you, neither does Sandi. We think you're made for each other.' Josie grinned. 'Now's your chance. You ought to take it. That's what it says in here to do.' Josie indicated the article she was reading. 'Take the initiative. I'll do the asking if you want me to,' she added.

Alex carefully marked the page in her book and put it down on the table.

'Look, Josie,' she said quietly, 'I don't care what it says in your trashy magazines, and I'm telling you this for the last time. I do not fancy him. And if you say anything to him, even one word, I'll kill you, and I mean it. I'll kill you very slowly. Now shut up and leave me alone. This is supposed to be silent reading.'

Alex picked up her book and found her place again but she still wasn't reading it. Something happening on Lauren Price's table had caught her attention.

In the classroom, they all had their own desks but these were pushed together in groups of four or five to form a table. Alex's was by the door. She sat next to Josie who had gone into a major huff now and had her back turned. The boys who sat opposite them were talking about computer games and leafing through a book about football. One of them looked up and winked, nodding towards Josie. Alex grinned at him. They were OK. You wouldn't hang round with them outside, but on the table you chatted together as you worked, told jokes, helped each other, playing games with bits of paper and rubbers when the lesson was boring, or Quaid wasn't looking. Minor squabbles broke out about people borrowing things but most of the time it was perfectly friendly.

But on Lauren Price's table it was different. Lauren sat by herself, staring at a book she obviously wasn't reading. The others had physically moved as far as they could away from her and were giggling to each other, as they busily constructed little barriers out of books and pencil cases like they were going to have a test or something.

But there were no tests scheduled for this morning. So it could only mean one thing. Lauren's table weren't speaking to her. They were sending her to Coventry.

Alex watched them on and off through the morning. Lauren didn't ask for help from any of them and no one was asking her. This was unusual, especially when they had maths. They weren't the smartest table in the room and Lauren was clever. They didn't borrow off her, or say one word to her, all the time Alex was watching.

The only time Alex saw anyone speak to her was as they passed on their way to the bin, or to get paper. They were delivering hate messages. Alex knew that's what they were doing by the way they whispered and the way, in spite of herself, Lauren flinched and blushed. Sometimes a note was dropped on her desk. Lauren didn't read them. She just screwed them up and carried on working.

So Lauren Price was the one they'd chosen. Why? OK, she was new to the school and she had no friends, but given the chance she'd probably make some, if she made the effort. She was not like Bailey, he'd been a natural for it. She was different. This kind of thing did not normally happen to someone like her. Alex would have sworn it.

Lauren stood against the wall at break, trying to make it look like she didn't care, but it wasn't working. When you're alone in a crowd you seem to stand out anyway, especially to yourself. It was like those dreams when you're walking down the street and all you have on is a vest.

Lunch-times were worse. She skirted the different groups running and playing, and stared at clusters of people laughing and talking, wearing her sullen indifference like a cloak to hide her unhappiness. In the dining hall, every mouthful seemed to take an hour to chew and she sat, self-conscious and silent in all the noise, staring at the contents of her lunch-box.

How long had this been going on? Alex wondered. Had it just started? Or had it been going on for some time but I was too wrapped up in myself to notice? Or maybe I did notice, she thought, but didn't want to see it. If she was honest that was nearer to it. Just like Bailey, she thought, and the truth stung painfully.

Alex hung around with Sandi and her mates at dinner-time, wandering the playground with them, part of the group. They didn't talk about it nonstop, it wasn't the sole topic of conversation, but every time they saw Lauren she came in for some comment or another.

'I can't stand her, she's a snob,' Josie said as they walked past where Lauren was standing.

'Nor me,' Andrea agreed. 'Stuck-up bitch. She's always going on about how great it was in Australia and how crap it is here.'

'Yeah,' Sandi said. 'Remember when she first came? She kept going on and on about how cool her old school was with loads of computers and an Olympic-size swimming pool.'

'And how she had millions of friends,' Josie chimed in, 'who all wore designer clothes and had pools of their own and hung out at the beach and went surfing just like in Beverly Hills.'

'Oh, yeah,' Andrea added, 'and don't forget about how the sun shone all the time and the weather was great and peaches and stuff grew in the garden and they had barbecues and parties and it was really wonderful . . .'

'Not like it is here!' they all chorused together.

'Mrs Dunbar did ask her to tell us what it was like in Australia,' Alex pointed out, reasonably.

'Yeah, well – she ought to go back there if it was all that brilliant,' Sandi said loud enough for her to hear.

'Look at her!' Andrea said, now they had attracted her attention. 'She's—'

Andrea stopped, sensing she wasn't the best-equipped person to attack someone else for their physical appearance. Lauren stared insolently back at her through slanting grey eyes. She knew she had the advantage there, at least over Andrea. Lauren was taller than most of the boys and slim. Her skin was still tanned and her short dark hair was well cut in a style that suited her strong clear features. She'd probably even look pretty if she smiled. I've only ever seen her really smile once, Alex realized.

'More like a boy than a girl!' Sandi sneered, coming to Andrea's rescue.

'Why don't you all go and—' Lauren shouted back.

Her last words were lost in siren wails as a group of little boys howled past, but they got the drift of what she was telling them to do.

'We don't use words like that here!' Sandi screamed over her shoulder as they walked away.

Alex had to grin at that one. Sandi swore more than anyone she knew. She used words even Helen didn't use.

They carried on attacking her and taking off her Australian accent even when she was well out of earshot. They went for everything, including the fact that her family had stopped off at Disneyland on the way over here.

'So what?' Alex said eventually. 'Adrian Green went to Orlando that time and you never got at him.'

'He didn't go on and on about it, though, did he?' Sandi said.

'She didn't go on and on about it,' Alex answered. 'She only mentioned it because Ms Quaid asked if anyone had been anywhere interesting. If I'd been there, I'd think it was pretty interesting. And Adie Green did go on and on about it. He wore that Mickey Mouse hat with the ears until it fell to pieces.'

'Anyway, it's different. He went to Florida. She went to San Francisco.'

'I don't see what that's got to do with anything,' Alex said, shaking her head.

'And she's stuck up. You can't deny that, Alex,'

Melanie Johnson, who was on Lauren's table, interrupted. 'She says she's done all the maths but she never offers to help any of us.'

They all looked at each other and nodded as though that clinched it.

'Yeah? So?' Alex folded her arms, feeling her temper rising. 'Did you ask her? Do you help her with anything? Do any of you even speak to her? I mean, why should she? It's not quite fair to—'.

'What's not fair, Alex?' Sandi asked and they all went quiet. 'Why are you sticking up for her?'

'I'm not—' Alex started to say, looking away.

'Sounds like it to me,' Sandi sneered. 'You haven't been the same, ever since Lisa went. You're always sucking up to Quaid, and all. You even sound like her. "It's not quite fair to . . ." ' Sandi folded her arms and looked down her nose, taking off Alex's words and expression. 'You're turning into a right little teacher's pet. Now Lisa's gone you better be careful – or you won't have any friends at all.'

Chapter 7

All through registration Alex brooded about what Sandi had said about being a teacher's pet.

No one had ever called her that before, although she'd been accused of practically everything else at one time or another. It was true she liked Ms Quaid more than other teachers, but that didn't necessarily make her a creep. Creeps were people who were always jumping about with their hands in the air as soon as the teacher opened her mouth, or scurrying around collecting things in and giving them out before anyone even asked them to.

It wasn't fair, Alex decided, it was a lie. But she nearly jumped a mile and blushed deeply when Ms Quaid came up behind her and put her hand on her shoulder.

'I'm putting up the wall display this afternoon, Alex,' the teacher said. 'And you've finished all your work, haven't you? I wonder if you would help me with it?'

Sandi and Andrea's we-were-right expressions made it a struggle for her not to shrug off the teacher's hand, but Alex managed to mumble, 'Yes, sure. Be happy to.'

The display area was outside the classroom by the far door. First they had to take down the old work and put up new backing paper, then Blu-Tack the new stuff on for Ms Quaid to come round later with the staple gun. Alex stood back to take a critical look as the teacher came out to see how they were getting on.

'Hey,' she said, 'that's looking pretty good.'

Alex and Josie smiled at the teacher's appreciation.

'We left a big space in the middle like you said, Miss.'

'What's it for?' Josie asked.

'It's for Lauren's kangaroo painting,' Ms Quaid replied, firing the staples into the soft board. 'I'll bring it out to you in a minute.'

She came back with a large sheet of black sugar paper and held it up in the space they'd left.

'There,' she said, grinning down at them, 'isn't that great!'

Two kangaroos bounded along together, one of them with a little one in its pouch. They had their heads turned as though they were looking straight at you. Their eyes were red, and the rest of them was outlined in white, filled in with a complex patterning of dots and stripes. The background was kind of deserty colours and the whole thing was surrounded by a thick border of abstract squirls and dashes.

Alex whistled, she'd never seen anything like it before. 'Wow!' she said. 'That's fantastic!'

Ms Quaid smiled. 'It's based on Aborigine art. You know, the original inhabitants of Australia, before the white people came? It's like their paintings.'

'I think it's a bit weird myself,' Josie said doubtfully. 'I mean, kangaroos are grey, aren't they? Not all stripy.'

'Oh, come on, Josie!' Alex protested. 'Anyone can see it's really good.'

'Art is a matter of taste, Alex.' Ms Quaid laughed, and then looked at her watch. 'Oh, God, is that the time? Come on, quick. You better go and get cleaned up. The bell will be going in a minute.'

As Alex made her way back to the classroom to collect her bag, she paused for a moment in the corridor to admire her afternoon's work and then stood absolutely still. The central panel, the painting of the two kangaroos, was missing. She looked around to see if it had fallen down. Nothing.

She went to tell Ms Quaid but she wasn't there. Then out of the window she saw Lauren. She was carrying what looked like two large sheets of black paper, one in each hand. Alex grabbed her things and dashed after her.

'Lauren, Lauren – wait!' she shouted. Lauren was near the big bins now. 'What are you doing?'

'What does it look like?' the other girl said as Alex approached. 'Getting rid of rubbish.'

'But why? Lauren, don't.' Alex grabbed her arm. 'It's your painting!'

'Yeah, I know. And look at it.' Lauren held it up for inspection. 'Some joker's been at it with a craft knife.'

Alex's face registered shock as she saw the jagged lines slashing through the animals that Lauren had so cunningly and carefully depicted. A clean zigzag cut the whole work in half.

The anger in Lauren's grey eyes was replaced by

despondency and the set line of her mouth wavered. She was close to tears.

'I've had it with this place,' she said as if to herself.

'Lauren, I'm really sorry. Your picture – it was really good.' Alex shook her head, not knowing what to say. 'That's a terrible thing for someone to do.'

'Oh, *you're* sorry! And I'm supposed to be grateful, am I?' Lauren spat the words out, angry that she had shown her emotions, revealed to one of them how hurt she was. 'Because you're sorry? Because you're not joining in with the other little snots? I don't give a stuff what you think.'

She pushed the ruined painting savagely into the bin and ran off towards the Infants' playground.

Alex stared after her and then turned, suddenly aware that there was someone behind her. David Morris was leaning against the wall, grinning.

'You ought to see your face, Alex,' he said. 'She certainly blew you out.'

Alex held her hands up in a gesture of despair and asked what he was doing there.

'I'm waiting for someone.'

'Who? Neil? He went ages ago.'

'No,' he said evasively. 'Someone else.'

'I hope it's not Sandi.' Alex laughed. 'You'd be wasting your time there. You've been well and truly dumped.'

'Yeah, I know,' he said, looking embarrassed. 'I wasn't waiting for her, anyway.'

'Who then?'

'You,' he said.

It was Alex's turn to blush.

'Oh,' she said and then her eyes narrowed. 'You

44

haven't been talking to Josie, have you?'

'No,' David shrugged, genuinely puzzled. He pushed himself off the wall. 'Might as well go. You coming?'

'Yeah,' Alex said.

'They've really got it in for her,' David said indicating Lauren, now with her sister, disappearing through the school gates.

'Looks like it,' Alex replied.

'Know why?'

Alex shook her head.

'Greg Simpson asked her out and she told him to get lost. That's what I heard.'

Alex stopped. 'Are you sure?'

'Straight up. One of his mates told me, he was cracking up about it. When she first came, Simpson really fancied her – so he asks her – and she just looks at him like he's dog dirt. He's not going to go for that, is he?'

No, he isn't, thought Alex. Neither is Sandi.

They carried on walking but Alex found it difficult to maintain their usual level of easy chat. Part of her mind was coming to terms with what he had just told her about Lauren. But another part was thinking about why he'd been waiting – for her, Alex.

She shot a glance at him when she thought he wasn't looking. He was carrying his tennis racquet, and the club was near Alex's house, that could be it. She found herself staring at him. She'd known him since Nursery, but he suddenly looked different. He'd just had his hair cut, it had been quite long and curly, now it was much shorter and looked darker, glinting and shining bronzy in the afternoon sun,

45

clipped close to his head. He tanned easily and his face was going brown. His eyes seemed bluer and she liked the way they crinkled up when he laughed. She realized he was laughing at her and went red, suddenly aware that her hair hadn't been brushed all day and she was bound to have ink or paint on her somewhere. What if she had B.O.? She couldn't smell anything, but you can't if it's yourself, Helen said. Is this what it means, she thought suddenly, to fancy somebody?

'What's the matter?' David was saying. 'Why are you walking way over there? And why are you staring at me like I'm an alien or something.'

'Nothing,' Alex mumbled. 'Sorry.'

'Will you water the plants while I'm away, then? And if it gets very hot move them out of the direct sun. I'd ask Neil but he'll only forget and I don't want them dying on me.'

'Yes, of course,' Alex agreed readily.

She liked the plants, they made the classroom more homelike and cheered the place up. David was in charge of their growing collection of specimens and was surprisingly knowledgeable about them.

'But where are you going?' she asked suddenly.

'Caravan in Great Yarmouth,' he laughed. 'I've just told you. I knew you weren't listening. We're going to this brilliant place. We've been there before. There's a games room, swimming pool, everything.'

'Sounds great,' she said, as they reached the traffic lights. 'How long are you going for?'

'Just the week. Shouldn't be going in the middle of term, really, but my mum cocked up her holiday dates.'

'Send me a postcard.'

He grinned. 'Wish you were here?'

'Something like that.' She grinned back.

He looked at his watch. 'I've got to go, Alex.' He slapped his leg with his tennis racquet. 'Got a lesson.'

'OK,' Alex said. 'See you, then.'

As she turned to go, he stopped her. 'I was thinking, you know, when I get back, I was wondering if you'd like a game some time? Tennis, I mean. We can play any time, my dad's taken out a family membership.'

Alex laughed loudly. 'Me? Play tennis? You've got to be joking! You know I'm hopeless. You're always going on about how hopeless I am!'

'It was just a thought.'

He turned away quickly, jabbing the button on the pelican lights. The little green man responded immediately.

'See you, Alex,' he said, and started off across the road.

He waved goodbye with his tennis racquet and went down Kingston Avenue in the direction of the tennis courts. Alex watched him go, calling herself every kind of idiot. She'd realized, seconds too late, that she was being asked out – like on a date. By then the words were out of her mouth and she'd blown it, probably hurting his feelings into the bargain. Sometimes even she couldn't believe she could be so stupid.

Chapter 8

The next day began with a full-scale inquest into Lauren's painting and what had happened to it. Ms Quaid was very upset, genuinely outraged that anyone would do that to someone else's work. But the class shrugged its shoulders, and muttered, 'I don't know', when she asked if anyone knew anything about it, and then kept stubbornly silent. She reacted by punishing all of them: cancelling their morning break and replacing afternoon Art and Craft with extra Maths.

The mood of the class deteriorated. Lauren had said nothing to Ms Quaid about what had happened. It was not her complaint that had led to their punishment, but she was the one they blamed for it.

'She grassed us up,' Greg said. 'Bet she took that blade to the picture herself.'

'Destroying her own work to gain attention,' Sandi whispered, 'and get us all into trouble. Just typical.'

The word went round and by the afternoon, as they sat under threat of detention, silently doing endless sums, resentment was burning deep in the class. A significant number of them, when told that Lauren had done it herself, were prepared to believe it.

Alex's pen slipped in her sweating hand as she stared at the bunches of numbers dancing about on the page. She felt slightly sick and had a blinding headache. It was all her fault. She'd gone to Ms Quaid and told her what had happened to Lauren's work as soon as she got to school. She'd thought it was the right thing to do, Quaid was bound to notice that the centrepiece of her wall display was missing. But when Lauren was asked into the classroom to discuss it, her slanted eyes had narrowed, inviting Alex to drop dead. She'd shrugged off the teacher's enquiries, saying, it didn't matter – what did she care?

Alex wanted to find a way to make it up to Lauren, or at least apologize to her for getting her into trouble with the rest of the class. But the other girl was becoming more hostile by the minute, busy setting up her own exclusion zone.

Alex started adding up the little clump of figures again. Every time she did the sum, it came out different. Her best bet was to wait until after three-thirty. Lauren and her sister, Caroline, were picked up by car, but their mother was often late. Alex had seen them waiting for her. She'd go over and just start talking. Lauren would have to stay and listen, if she walked off she'd miss her mother.

After school, she followed Lauren out of the gates. It was important to avoid making a complete mess of things, like she'd done with David yesterday night. He'd left early for his holiday and, although he'd been friendly enough this morning when he'd handed over the plant-care box and issued his last-minute instructions to her, she'd hurt him and she knew it. And she was missing him already. Alex was beginning to get the feeling she was going to need every friend she'd got.

She crossed the road towards the Price sisters, this

time she had to get it right. By talking to Quaid, she'd managed to turn the whole class against Lauren. In her head she heard the voice of her sister, saying: 'Alex, when are you going to learn to keep that big mouth shut?'

Chapter 9

'I'm at Lauren Price's house. You know, the girl you asked me about yesterday. Is it OK if I stay for tea? Her mum's invited me.'

Alex shifted the phone to her other ear and looked at the pictures on the wall of the unfamiliar hall. For once things were working out well.

'Yes, she is. Very. No, of course I won't. Anyway, it's Friday. Thanks, Mum. See you later.'

'My mum says it's OK, I can stay,' she said as she returned to the kitchen.

'That's super, Alex.' Lauren's mother smiled at her from over by the sink. Lauren sat at the table scowling. 'We're having pasta with a kind of tomatoey sauce, do you like it?'

'Yes, Mrs Price, that sounds fine.' Alex smiled back nervously, awkward in the face of Lauren's hostility. 'I don't want to put you to any trouble. I like anything, really.'

'It's no trouble, I told you, and we've got absolute heaps.'

Lauren's mother was quite young and very attractive, with a smiling, open face and friendly grey eyes. She was pushing back coils and strands of thick shiny dark hair and re-twisting her rough chignon with long-fingered, slim brown hands. She was tall and

51

slender, like Lauren, but her accent was different. Sharper, more pronounced, more Australian.

'It's so nice to have Lauren inviting friends back,' she was saying.

'I didn't invite her. You did,' Lauren muttered through clenched teeth.

Alex and Mrs Price grinned at each other, embarrassed, as Lauren's scowl deepened.

'I like any kind of pasta,' Alex said in a rush, 'anything Italian, you know, spaghetti, and, er, lasagne,' she searched her mind for other names, 'and that stuff in big fat tubes, what's it called?'

'Cannelloni,' Lauren supplied.

'Yes.' Alex smiled in relief. 'I like that too. Anything, honest, Mrs Price.'

'Well, that's good.' Lauren's mother dried her hands on a tea-towel and picked up a knife. 'And not so much of the Mrs Price stuff. I'd like you to call me Jenny. Will you promise?'

Alex nodded quickly and looked away. She was not used to calling people's mothers by their first names.

'Now, Lauren. Why don't you take your guest upstairs while I get on with the cooking?'

'Do I have to?' Lauren asked sulkily but got no reply. Her mother had started chopping onions with the speed and skill of a chef. 'Oh, all right. Come on, then.'

She got up and left the kitchen, indicating for Alex to follow her with a curt flick of the head.

Alex went up the stairs, thinking how strange it was to be there at all. She had been standing outside school, trying to get Lauren to talk to her, when Mrs Price pulled up. Before she knew what was happening, Lauren's mother was clearing the back seat of her little car and inviting her home to have tea with them. She shrugged off Alex's polite protests, and Lauren's more serious ones, with such relentless good nature that eventually they gave up and Alex scrambled over the tipped-up passenger seat, squeezing in next to Caroline.

The nameplate on Lauren's door had various additions executed in felt-tip. The sweet little girl had a mass of spiky black hair and long sharp fangs dripping blood. A Garfield notice, swinging from the handle, snarled, 'NO PARENTS BEYOND THIS POINT'.

Alex followed Lauren into the room and then stood still, arrested by the wall opposite. In the middle was a floor-to-ceiling poster of a surfer, crouched and curled on a big bright board, under a huge, curving, blue-green glassy wave. The top sparkled like crystal, shattering onto the surfer's bronzed shoulders.

That was impressive but what had stopped Alex in her tracks were the framed pictures on either side. They were like Lauren's painting, the one that had been destroyed. These were in brilliant black and white, or subdued earthy colours: oranges, yellows, the red of dried blood. There were human figures, some long and thin, others squat and fat, with strangely distorted elongated heads and huge feet that made them look magical and alien. Alex liked the animals best. They were not at all realistic but each one was recognizable as a lizard or a crocodile, brought into instant life by the flick of a tail or the angle of the head.

'You like my surfer?' A ghost of a smile crossed

Lauren's face. She was enjoying the impression her room was making. 'Great, isn't she? All-Australian Champion.'

'Yes,' Alex replied, 'but I like those pictures more. I've never seen anything like them, except yours.'

'They're Aboriginal. Done by native Australian artists. My dad took me to an exhibition in Perth. I stayed all day, he couldn't get me away until he'd bought some for me. They aren't originals, of course. Just posters.'

She threw herself down on a nest of big bright cushions and indicated for Alex to join her.

Alex sat down and hugged her knees, still staring at the pictures.

'You know,' she said, 'my mum would love them.'

'Oh, yeah.' Lauren played with a tassel, plaiting and replaiting it. 'Why's that? She an Art teacher or something?'

'Yeah, she teaches at the college. She does work of her own too, when she gets the time.'

'Yeah?' Lauren was beginning to sound interested. 'I kind of . . .' she started to say and then she broke off, changing the subject. 'My mum works too. Guess what she does?'

Alex smiled and shrugged. She couldn't. She didn't know her well enough.

'See her chopping those onions? Fastest chopping in the west. She cooks, she's a chef.'

'Really?'

'Yeah. She's working mornings and lunch-times in one of the restaurants in town. Back home . . .' She paused again and corrected herself. 'When we lived in Australia, she had her own place. Ran it with her friend. They were partners.'

Alex was surprised at how well the conversation was going, relieved that they were getting on at all if she was honest, when Lauren deliberately turned away and fell silent. Alex looked round frantically for something else to talk about when she saw them. Perched on the nose of a ferocious-looking mask were Sandi's pink polka-dot sunglasses.

'You've got some amazing stuff,' she remarked, clearing her throat. 'Where did all those masks come from?'

The wall above the bed was covered in them, all different shapes and sizes. Some were smooth and bland except for their bright painted colours, others were tusked and fanged with tongues sticking out in terrifying grimaces.

'Oh,' Lauren replied, not even glancing at them. She was studying Alex instead. 'Malaysia, Indonesia, Bali, Hong Kong. Different places.'

'Have you been to them all?' Alex asked.

She was trying not to stare but the sunglasses loomed huge, heightening the tension between them.

'Not all. I've been to Bali on holiday, and Indonesia, but my dad brought me the rest back when he went on business trips.'

'What does he do, your dad?' Alex asked, tearing her eyes away from the wall and trying to get back into an ordinary conversation.

'He works in computers.'

'Oh, who for?'

'For a big international firm, that's why we're here,' Lauren exclaimed impatiently. 'What are you doing here? What do you want, Alex?'

'I'm here because your mum invited me . . .' Alex started to say.

'Bull!' Lauren exclaimed impatiently. 'You followed me out of school. You were watching me all day. What do you want from me? If it's a set-up, masterminded by Sandi and her cruddy little friends, I'm warning you, I've just about had enough, I'll—'

'No.' Alex held up her hands. 'It's nothing like that. I promise. It's just that I – I wanted to apologize about this morning. I thought it was wrong – what happened to your painting. But maybe I shouldn't have told Quaid, without asking you. I'm sorry.'

Lauren's face was closed and inscrutable, but fierce at the same time, like one of the masks on the wall behind her.

'Yeah,' she said, her grey eyes hard and flinty. 'You should learn to mind your own business. I might have done it myself – like they're saying. Might have stolen those too, for all you know.' She nodded towards the masks with a harsh little laugh. 'Look at you, can't keep your eyes off them, can you? I know what you're thinking.'

Alex shook her head. 'No, you don't,' she said.

'Dob on me about them as well, why don't you?' Lauren sneered.

'I don't tell on people,' Alex said evenly. 'How did you get them, Lauren?'

'Maybe I did steal them, to get even with the little cow . . .' Lauren sighed, suddenly her anger subsided. 'But I didn't. They were in my bag. I found them.'

Alex nodded. It figured. That's what they'd been up to on Wednesday afternoon. The sunglasses had been planted to make it look like Lauren had stolen them, but the plan went wrong when Ms Quaid refused to allow a full-scale search to be carried out. She explained her theory to Lauren.

'Yes, that's what I thought, too,' the other girl said. 'You don't have to be a genius to work that one out.' She reached up and swiped them off the mask. 'I mean, what would I want with these? Look!' She perched them on the end of her nose. Alex laughed. 'They are *really* tacky.'

'Maybe we should take them to Quaid,' Alex said. 'Try to explain . . .'

'No!' Lauren swept the glasses off.

'She won't think you took them or anything . . .'

'No, she'll make a big fuss and make it all worse.' Lauren shook her head. 'You saw what she was like this morning. So. Not one word. I mean it!' She stared intently at Alex for a moment and then looked away. 'I don't want it getting back to my mum. She's got enough worries.'

'OK.' Alex shrugged. 'If that's how you feel about it.'

'Yes, that's how I feel about it.'

'They'll try to use them again, you know.' Alex picked up the glasses, twirling them around.

'Let them.' Lauren's voice was muffled by her knees. 'I don't care.'

'Maybe . . .'

'Maybe what?' Lauren looked up at Alex.

'Nothing, just an idea.' Alex stood up and put them back on the mask. 'They're safe enough there for the moment.'

Lauren sat hugging her knees, her face hidden. The sullen resignation that Alex sensed beneath the sudden bursts of defiant hostility made her feel helpless. She recognized, with a certain amount of surprise, that she could genuinely get to like Lauren. She knew things, had been to places and done things, that suddenly made all the other people Alex knew seem boring, made Alex want to know more about her.

There was no way at the moment of explaining any of this, Alex reflected gloomily in the lengthening silence. In fact, it didn't look as if they would ever speak again, Lauren seemed to have cut herself off so completely.

'Lauren? You've got to come down now. Mum says tea's ready.'

Caroline, Lauren's younger sister, came into the room and stared at Alex with open curiosity. She was small for her age, thin and slight and, although about eight years old, looked much younger. Long strands of baby-fine fair hair wisped out from a very long plait, framing her thin elfin face in a misty halo. She was wearing one of the weirdest collections of clothes Alex had ever seen. A Laura Ashley pinafore dress billowing out over an outsize T-shirt and floral leggings and on her feet were a pair of very small, unlaced Doc Martens.

'OK, OK. Tell her we're coming.' Lauren wiped a hand over her face as though she had been asleep and got up from her sitting position without using her hands.

Alex tried the same thing and toppled over.

Caroline laughed. 'You've got to practise that,' she said. 'It's yoga.'

Alex came downstairs from the oppressive silence of

Lauren's bedroom, trying to think of ways of getting out of staying, but the smell of food changed her mind. Maybe she'd eat before she went, it would be rude not to after Mrs Price had gone to all that trouble, and she was starving.

The food was really good and there was plenty of it. Mrs Price chatted to Alex in her breezy way, asking easy questions about herself and her family until Alex felt more relaxed and began to enjoy herself.

Caroline talked a lot as well. It was only Lauren who sat saying little, pushing food around her plate, responding only to requests to pass this or that, making no attempt to join in any of the conversation.

Caroline had a surprisingly deep, gruff voice and a wide variety of strongly held opinions. She had to be stopped by her mother from dominating everything. Just like Helen, Alex thought, the two of them should get together. Like Helen too, Caroline enjoyed telling stories.

'Makes them all up,' Lauren remarked acidly. 'All total fantasy.'

'I don't!' Caroline said, glaring at her sister. 'Anyway, this one's true. Gemma and Tammy were telling me today. It's about this kid called Bailey . . .'

Alex nearly choked on a mouthful of pudding and gulped at her drink to help it down.

'Yeah,' Caroline continued, ignoring the interruption. Her pale eyes narrowing and glittering with excitement. 'He used to go to the school and something terrible happened to him. He died in a real horrible way – he fell down off that footbridge thingy near the school, right on to the road, and the cars went over and over him until he was all squidged out and spread around like strawberry jam—'

'That's enough, Caroline!' Her mother held up her hand. 'You know I don't like you talking that way at the dinner table.'

'That's the way they told it, Mum!' Caroline replied indignantly. 'Anyway, not all the stories are like that. One says he fell on top of a lorry, and he bounced around but he didn't fall off, and it took him far, far away and no one ever saw him again. Not in real life, anyway,' she added, 'but Gemma and Tammy don't believe that. They think he died and turned into a ghost.' She looked around the table, and lowered her husky voice to a dramatic whisper. 'He lives there, at the school. He's been seen loads of times, by tons of people. The school's got its very own ghost. Don't you think that's cool? I've even been shown where his home is.'

Caroline sat back and surveyed them, to see the impact this information was having.

'Certainly sounds interesting,' her mother commented. 'Alex, can you tell us any more about this?'

Alex told them what she knew of the stories, corrected on nearly every detail by Caroline.

'But it's not true, any of it,' Alex finished.

'It is!' Caroline insisted. 'Plenty of people have seen him. Plenty. And I believe them, not you!'

'Caroline!' her mother said sharply. 'We don't speak that way to guests.'

'And she's my guest too,' Lauren said, 'so you better shut up. Go on, Alex.'

'It can't be true because he isn't dead . . .'

'How do you know?' Caroline interrupted rudely.

'I know because . . .'

At that moment the phone rang. Whatever Alex

was going to say was lost in the scramble to answer it.

'It's Dad, he'll be late. His meeting's going on longer than expected,' Mrs Price told them when she returned.

'What time will he be back?' Caroline demanded.

Her mother shrugged. 'He doesn't know, but he says don't wait up.'

The news didn't go down too well and from Caroline's angry howl of disappointment and Lauren's brooding look, Alex got the idea that this was often happening. Mrs Price sighed and looked at her watch.

'Would you like a lift home, Alex?'

Chapter 10

Alex woke up, automatically registered it was Saturday, closed her eyes and turned over, willing sleep to come back, but it was too late. Bright morning light spilled in all round the window blind, the Hoover buzzed away downstairs, Helen's radio blared next door and Jack set up extra loud purring now he knew that she was awake.

Her unfocused thoughts drifted back to last night. In the Prices' car, Alex had felt tired, relieved to be going home. Although she liked Lauren, she wasn't easy to be with and if what they had was friendship, it was still at the stage where one false move could kill it off altogether. Alex was even less sure of Caroline, and although Mrs Price was really nice, sometimes it seemed to be only her mouth that was smiling, her eyes stayed worried. Like Mum, Alex thought, when she wants you to think she's happy and on top of the world, but she's feeling just the opposite. There was a tension in their house, something always there but unspoken, that made Alex's family seem quite relaxed, almost normal.

When she got in, everyone had seemed glad to see her. Helen was in one of her generous and friendly moods. She had just bought a nail varnish kit and offered to do Alex's and didn't make any sarcastic comments about bitten stubby nails. Dad asked her where she'd been and actually listened when she told him, and Mum was really interested in Lauren and her Aboriginal paintings.

'You'll have to invite her for tea,' she said. 'I'd like to meet her. How about one day next week?'

Alex had readily agreed but was glad her mother hadn't said tomorrow. It was nice to have time on your own, to think about the things that had happened.

Like going to Lauren's house and the feeling she'd had in that strange room, among the masks and the paintings, of discovering something new, of things beginning. Suddenly a new thought came into her head. Sandi's sunglasses. They filled her mind, large and black, upswept pink rims polka-dotted. Perched on that hideous mask, and then on Sandi's nose, and then Andrea showing off, her own glasses eclipsed by them. They had planted them on Lauren deliberately, to get her into trouble. It wasn't enough just thinking, or even talking. Whatever Lauren said, people shouldn't get away with stuff like that, something should be done about it.

When she heard Helen clatter downstairs and bang the front door on her way to her clarinet class, Alex slid out of bed and went into her sister's room. She picked her way carefully through the chaos and then sat down cross-legged on the floor, having found what she came in for.

'Alex? Alex! Have you been in my room?'

Helen marched in, seized Alex by the shoulder and shook her.

'No, of course not. What would I want to go in

that tip for?' Alex lied indignantly. 'And let me go or I'll tell Mum.'

Helen dropped her and Alex dodged out of reach.

'You have,' Helen insisted, glowering down at her. 'I can tell, so don't bother lying. You've been in there going through my *Just Seventeen*s.'

'How could you tell? An army could march through and you wouldn't be able to tell the difference.'

'That's where you're wrong.' Helen grinned triumphantly. 'It's obsessively neat little people like you who can't tell the difference. It's my mess and I know every bit of it. I could come in here any time and you'd never know.' She looked round Alex's tidy room contemptuously. 'Not that there's anything worth finding.' She went to the box where Alex kept her private things and flipped it open. 'Why don't you ever finish your letters to Lisa? And who,' she said, holding up a piece of paper covered in connected names and doodled hearts, 'exactly is David?'

Alex flew at her sister. Helen laughed and held her off with one hand, then flipped her round, putting an arm lock on her. 'So what were you doing in my magazines, then?' Helen hissed as she tightened her hold. 'Huh? Huh?'

'I was just looking for something!' Alex gasped out.

Helen let her go and she catapulted across the floor.

'Oh, yeah? Like what?'

'Nothing.' The long arm snaked out again and Alex quickly said, 'Something we're doing for school – about bullying!'

'Find anything?' Helen was still regarding her suspiciously.

'Yeah. Some.' Alex rubbed her arm, still wincing.
'Any help?'

'A bit.'

The suspicion on Helen's face settled into certainty. 'I think you should tell Mum.'

'Why?' Alex asked, genuinely mystified.

'Because she ought to know.' Helen folded her arms and frowned down at her sister. 'I thought there was something up. I nearly said so the other night when I found you crying.'

Alex stared at her in astonishment and then started grinning.

'It's not about me, honestly Helen. It's someone else.'

'Oh, come off it.' Helen's frown deepened. 'It's not me, it's my friend? You won't put me off that easily.'

'It isn't me. I swear it. It's that new girl from Australia. The one I had tea with last night. The one I was telling you about.'

Helen looked away, embarrassed. 'Oh, right. I didn't like to think about it happening to you, that's all. I was, well, kind of worried.'

Helen went towards the door and then turned back. 'Alex?'

'Yes?' She looked up from the magazine she had been hiding.

'Doesn't matter what they say in *Just Seventeen*. Keep out of it or they'll start on you. That's my advice.'

Late in the afternoon, Alex had just got back from the library with a pile of books when the phone rang. Her mother answered it and shouted from the hall.

'It's for you, Alex!'

'Oh, hello, is that Alex?' It was a woman's voice. 'Jenny – Mrs Price here – Lauren's mum?'

'Oh, hello. Yes, it's me – Alex.'

'Sorry to bother you. But . . .' Mrs Price paused for a moment, and then asked quickly, 'Are Lauren and Caroline with you, by any chance?'

'No, I'm afraid not.' Alex stopped, trying to think. The question was casual enough but Mrs Price sounded worried. 'I haven't seen them, sorry.'

'Oh, I just thought they might . . .' The voice trailed off.

'What's happened, Mrs Price? Can I help?'

'Well, Lauren went out looking for Caroline and they should have been back ages ago.' She was still trying to disguise it, but Alex could hear the fear and concern in her voice. 'And frankly I'm rather worried.'

'Where did they go?' Alex asked.

'Some friends of Caroline's came round for her earlier to go to the park. And then it was getting a little late so Lauren went down there to look for her, but neither of them have come back.'

'They could be round at someone's house,' Alex said. 'Do you know who the friends were? I might know where they live.'

'Gemma and Tammy, but both of them are home, I've just phoned their parents. They have no idea where my two are . . . I thought they just might have dropped in on you on your way back . . .'

'No . . .'

'Sorry to bother you, then, Alex. Tell them to come straight home if they do turn up.'

'Yes, OK . . .' Alex began but Mrs Price had rung off before she could finish the sentence.

Alex thought about her worrying at home, remembering all the times she'd been with Lisa, deep in some game or other, losing all track of time, while their mothers went frantic.

'I'm going out again, Mum,' she shouted as she grabbed her coat. 'I'll be back in a bit.'

Alex set off on her bike towards school, after dismissing the park as a possibility. Tammy James and her sister Elaine lived in a house that backed on to the playground. Alex recalled Caroline's stories of the night before, she knew where she'd got them from. The James sisters were a bit on the weird side and were the self-appointed guardians of the ghost of Michael Bailey.

She dismounted automatically as she rounded the corner of the First School building.

The yard stretched out in front of her, huge and empty. Shadows from the buildings and trees were crowding and lengthening across it. The only sound was the squeak of her tyres and her own breathing. She started across the familiar place as she had so many times before but her bike wheels ticked loud and her footsteps, normally deadened by the sound of a thousand other feet, rang out and echoed alarmingly. She stopped. To go on would increase her sudden feeling of being exposed, picked out. The hair crept on the back of her neck and she instinctively avoided any sound or movement that might further alert some secret watcher in the shadows, who might be there, waiting for her.

She stood undecided, looking around the

67

perimeter. She'd never noticed, when the place was full of people, how the crooks and quirks of the buildings created so many corners and hidden places, all now deeply shaded. She could almost hear the hidden presence whispering and sniggering at her.

A car horn sounded loud in a nearby street and broke the eerie silence. She stepped forward.

'Alex, Alex!'

She stopped dead when she heard it, and then it came a second time. A thin, clear voice calling her name. She stared ahead, not daring to move. There it was again. It seemed inside her and outside her at the same time. Not her voice, or like she was imagining it, but the voice of another person. A high-pitched boy's voice. She had not heard it for years, but she knew it instantly. It was Michael Bailey.

Chapter 11

'Alex? Alex!'

This time it was a girl's voice, warm and human. She could feel breath on her cheek and a hand shaking her shoulder.

'Are you all right? What are you doing just standing here? What's the matter?'

Alex turned slowly and stiffly, as if in a dream, and faced Lauren. She wanted to hug her, cling on to her, telling her fear, but she didn't.

Instead, she said: 'You mum phoned, she was worried about you and Caroline. Thought you might be at my place. But you weren't. I had an idea where Caroline might be, so I came here.'

She told Lauren about the James sisters and the Bailey stories as they wheeled their bikes across the playground. It all feels quite normal, Alex thought, now Lauren's here all the strangeness has gone.

'Yeah,' Lauren said, 'you could be right. Caroline loves that kind of stuff. She keeps all sorts of weird junk like that hidden in her room, including a Ouija board. Mum'd flip out if she knew. She thinks it's just Caro's vivid imagination.' Lauren laughed and shook her head. 'Most of the time Caro's not even on this planet.'

They went to the back of the school and on to the

access road that led along the rear of the opposite houses. Neither of them said anything but they were heading towards Bailey's garage. The last long shafts of sun extended like fingers along the centre of the dusty track, picking out ridges and ruts in sharp relief, casting their walking shapes into ungainly elongated shadows. The sun disappeared behind a line of houses and the light went quickly, as if someone had flicked a switch. The dark shapes at their sides seemed to be merging and losing their outlines, so they could no longer be identified as bushes, bins and straggling trees. The two girls instinctively moved closer together.

They were near the garage now, approaching it cautiously, when there was a sharp noise to the left. They stopped, clutching onto each other, as a small black and white cat scooted out in front of them. He sat for a moment, licking furiously at his ruffled fur, and then bolted again at a sound only he could hear.

'Look at him,' Lauren said, 'having a quick wash, pretending he's not bothered.'

They both laughed.

Then Alex grabbed Lauren's arm. 'Do you hear that?' she asked, her voice dropping to a whisper.

Lauren nodded. They both stood absolutely still, listening to a deep rhythmic thump, thumping. It was resonant and muffled at the same time, like a big sound coming from far away but the source was actually very near. The two girls turned to stare at the caretaker's garage.

One of the big bins on wheels stood right up against the rotting doors and it sounded like someone trapped inside was kicking against it. A thin voice cried:

'Let me out! Let me out!'

Lauren leapt up, catching hold of the side of the bin. She hung there for a moment, trying to peer into the garage.

'It's Caroline!' she shouted. 'Help me, Alex!'

She jumped down and the two of them manoeuvred the heavy bin out of the way. Caroline came wriggling out of the hole at the bottom of the door. She came out feet first, pink leggings and dress covered in dust, her face streaked with dirt and her long fair hair, full of bits of paint and wood, snagged and tangled.

Lauren helped her up and began brushing her down. Caroline didn't answer any of her sister's questions but stood more or less obediently until Lauren started rubbing at her face with a spit-covered handkerchief.

'Just a minute,' she said and wrestled herself out of Lauren's grip.

She was disappearing back into the garage like a weasel down a rabbit hole when Lauren hauled her out by the seat of her leggings.

'Caroline! What the hell do you think you're doing?'

'I've left my Ouija board in there, Lauren,' Caroline cried, struggling furiously. 'I've got to get it.'

'Oh, no you don't.' Lauren pulled her roughly to her feet and held her by the scruff of her neck. 'It's staying in there. You're not going to get it, and you're not going to play with one ever again. Do you hear?'

'I'll make another one,' Caroline said defiantly and then suddenly all the fight went out of her. She slumped against her sister's shoulder and started to cry.

'Hey,' Lauren said softly, leading her away. 'It's OK. We're here now. You want to tell us what happened?'

Caroline snuffled and wiped her nose on her sleeve. She looked up, tears spiking her pale lashes and her big eyes all pupil. She stared at Alex, as though it was the first time she'd noticed anyone else there besides Lauren.

'It's all right, Caro. Alex is my friend. Yours too. She showed me where to find you.'

Alex tried to smile in a reassuring way but Caroline's look was far from trustful.

'How did she know where I was? For all you know she could have been one of them.'

Alex was about to protest but Lauren motioned her to be quiet.

'One of who, Caro?' she asked, putting her arm round her sister.

'One of the kids who blocked me in there, half of them are in her class. That tall tarty one with the blonde hair and her ugly little mate with the glasses.' Caroline sniffed. 'Couple of scrags. And there were some boys too, but I don't know them. We saw them in the playground. Then I heard them outside, they must have followed. They were giggling and laughing. They let Tammy out but not me. They pushed that big bin thing up against the entrance.'

'But what were you doing in there in the first place?' Lauren asked.

72

'Me and Tammy had this idea. To use the Ouija to talk to Michael Bailey.' She wiped her eyes with her shirt. 'Would have worked too, if they hadn't interrupted. They thought I'd be scared. I heard them talking, that's why they did it. But I wasn't. I knew Michael wouldn't hurt me. But then it was getting dark and I thought I'd be there all night and Mum and Dad would worry and if they found out about the Ouija board I'd get into all kinds of trouble. I was so glad when you came, Lo. You won't tell them, will you?'

Lauren hugged her for a moment and then let her go.

'No,' she said, 'but on one condition. No more Ouija boards. If I find out you're messing with it again – or any of that stuff, I'll go straight to Mum and I mean it.'

'OK.' Caroline managed a smile. 'It's a deal.'

They crossed the playground and said goodbye at the gates. Alex glanced back before she set off home. The place looked strange at night, unfamiliar, bathed in a peculiar grey pink by the security lights. Maybe there was no Bailey ghost, but there could have been. She thought of the throngs who would be there Monday morning. If ever a set of people deserved haunting, they did.

Chapter 12

Alex Lewis would not normally be included among those very few people who actually like Monday mornings, but today she felt wide awake as soon as her eyes opened and lay in bed grinning to herself. Her life since Lisa left had been like a trudge from day to day, all shades of grey, now it was splashed with colour. There were things to look forward to and say 'I can't wait' about. Like getting to school and seeing Lauren. She had phoned on Sunday afternoon and they had talked on and on into the early evening. It was as though they only had one call to get to know each other and, when Alex finally put down the receiver, she knew she had found a friend.

Her good mood held all morning. She had someone to chat to in the line before school and they walked into Assembly together. Alex asked to go to the library with Lauren first lesson and at break they stayed and played with each other. Curious eyes were on them and the rustle of whispering accompanied them everywhere but, for once, Alex didn't mind being the centre of attention. Things were different now. Let them stare.

Alex was smiling to herself, holding a place in the dinner queue for Lauren, when she felt a kick to the back of the knees and an arm across her shoulders sent her crashing into the wall. She heard

Greg Simpson's voice and felt his breath hot on her ear as he ground her face into the brick.

'Get to the back of the queue, Lewis, and stay there. I hope you enjoy what you get.' He hitched her arm further up her back. 'Because if you don't stop hanging around with that Australian bitch, you'll be paying all your dinner money to me, and this'll be the last time you eat here.'

After he had delivered his warning, Greg Simpson slightly relaxed his hold. Alex's quick, sharp, backwards jab took him by surprise and he doubled over, letting go of her as the hard elbow sank into the soft flesh under his ribs. She whirled round but the knee she was aiming between his legs missed. He grabbed her leg and they toppled over.

Alex had really lost her temper now and the ferocity of her attack took him by surprise, but in the end her blind fury was no match for his superior weight and strength. He had her pinned down and was bending the fingers of her right hand back, screaming in her face for submission. The pain was acute. Alex felt the tears of defeat filling her throat, when the grip he had on her slackened.

From far away she heard a scream that wasn't hers, and a voice saying:

'Let her up, Simpson.' The scream became a prolonged thin wail. 'I mean it!' the voice said.

Greg's hold on Alex slackened further. She blinked away the tears and gradually everything swam into focus. Lauren was standing there, with Sandi's long fair hair wrapped round one hand. She was pulling so hard Sandi's head was snapped right back and her throat bulged.

'Let her up, I said.' Lauren kicked Greg hard on

the thigh to gain his full attention. 'You let go of Alex or I'll pull your girlfriend's hair out chunk by chunk.' She gave the silky blonde hair a further vicious twist. 'I mean it. She's gonna be bald by the time I've finished!'

The skin was pulled so hard, Sandi's eyes were slits. Tears oozed from them, the pain was genuine.

'Please, Greg. Please!' she sobbed out. 'Get her off me!'

Alex was released and scrambled to her feet massaging the feeling back into her fingers. When she was free and clearly all right, Lauren released Sandi. A contemptuous shove in the back pitched her forward into Greg's arms.

'Here you are!' she yelled. 'I don't know what you want her for, stupid little—'

'All right, break it up, break it up.' The fat dinner lady was bustling through now. 'What's going on here?' She grabbed hold of Lauren and then let go of her, shocked by the furious words that greeted her interference. 'You better come with me. Straight to the Head. We don't use language like that, young lady!'

'I saw everything, Mrs Thomas,' Andrea piped up. 'It was Alex and Lauren, they started the whole thing . . .'

'Shut up, Four Eyes,' Lauren growled.

'That's enough!' the dinner lady barked at Lauren. 'Are you all right, dear?' Her tone changed quickly to concern as she gave a tissue to the sniffling Sandi. 'I don't know, girls fighting like the boys now.' She sighed, hands flapping to show her disgust and despair. 'You two are coming with me.' She hauled

Alex and Lauren roughly to her side. 'You better come too, dear,' she said, putting a protective arm round Sandi. 'And you, Greg Simpson.'

They trailed along after her, Andrea coming as well as a witness. Ms Quaid was summoned from the staffroom and went in to see the Head. They had to go in one by one, and spent the rest of dinner-time sitting outside his office.

'That's just so typical!' Lauren was snorting with indignation. 'All I was doing was trying to help you and I'm getting a letter sent home. For Christ's sake! I'm the one who's getting bullied!'

'We've all got letters, Lauren,' Alex said despondently. 'And you shouldn't have sworn at the dinner lady.'

She just wanted to go home at the end of a day that had started so well and ended so badly. All the hope she'd felt earlier had disappeared. Lauren was being like she was before, hating everything, full of sullen resentment. She was hitting out at everybody, Alex included. Their friendship was still too new and delicate to take this much of a pounding.

'It's true, then,' she said as they walked along the corridor.

'What is?'

'What they say about Australians,' Alex said with a half smile, trying to cheer her up, 'not giving a 4X.'

'Shut up, Alex. That's not funny.' Lauren's voice rose higher, she was near to tears. 'Everyone here swears all the time. Every last one, swearing like troopers, mouths like sewers, but that's OK, the teachers don't hear it. Just because it's me . . .' she kicked viciously at the wall. 'This place. They're such a load of hypocrites. I hate it, hate it, hate it!'

'Alex, Lauren!' Ms Quaid was shouting to them from the classroom door. 'I'd like a word with you. Can you come back here a minute?'

'Lauren.'

No response.

'I think I know what's been going on.'

Still no response.

'Lauren.' Ms Quaid's voice dropped, quiet and kind. 'I know what they're doing, I've got eyes in my head. I know what you've been going through. Now, do you want to tell me about it?'

Lauren flicked the hair out of her eyes but continued staring straight ahead. She hadn't said a word since they'd entered the classroom.

The teacher sighed in the silence and fiddled with the pens on her desk.

'What happened at dinner-time isn't the best way of handling it, though, is it?' she said finally. 'If you act like them, you'll only end up getting hurt, or getting into even more trouble. And, and' – she leaned forward with both arms on the table, her hands held out in appeal – 'I can't get the Head to take what's been happening to you seriously, if he thinks you're just as bad as they are, can I? Can I, Lauren?'

Lauren sat on, not even acknowledging that she'd heard the question. Ms Quaid watched her intently and when Alex cleared her throat in readiness to say something, anything, to break the terrible stretching silence, the teacher motioned her to be quiet.

Tears were sliding from the corners of Lauren's closed eyes. They ran down her face and along the side of her nose, dripping off her chin to make dark splashes on her blue sweatshirt. No sobs or gulps accompanied the long steady flow. Lauren could weep soundlessly, as though she'd practised it.

Finally with a soft sort of hiccough she stopped. She wiped her face on her sleeve and groped in her pocket.

'I'm sorry,' she murmured, as if to herself. 'I'm sorry.'

Ms Quaid reached into her drawer. Alex could feel tears pricking behind her own eyes and gathering in her throat, as she took the box of tissues and handed them to Lauren. The teacher came round her desk and put her arm round the girl and held her for a moment.

'Don't cry now. You're not on your own, you know. You've got me, and you've got Alex here. It's going to stop – right now. I promise.'

Chapter 13

'Do you know what I hate most,' Lauren was saying. 'What I really hate most about it?'

Lauren squinted down and Alex shook her head. They were crossing the canal bridge, on their way to Lauren's house.

'I hate the way they're making me into someone else. I never felt like that before. I was never like that in my old school.' She shrugged and pushed her hands deeper in her pockets. 'When you come to a new place, and you don't know anyone, it kind of really knocks your confidence. It was like they're turning me into someone I don't even recognize. A different person.'

'What's that?' Alex stopped suddenly, distracted from Lauren's words by a movement up ahead. She looked behind quickly, just to make sure. She held Lauren's arm and whispered.

'Keep walking but slow right down. I think we're about to be ambushed.'

'What?' Lauren said, puzzled, looking around.

'Up there.' Alex indicated with a nod of her head. 'By those new houses. As soon as we're across here drop down onto the cycleway.'

Lauren peered ahead, eyes narrowed. A group of kids, three or four, half obscured by the flimsy fly-postered boarding. They had pieces of wood from the building site. One of them bashed away at a tree with his, the others were having a mock sword fight.

'The two sword fighting are the Riley twins,' Alex said. 'The other one is Malc Conway.'

'So?'

'So, they're Bridge Boys.' Alex turned round casually. 'And coming up behind is Greg and the rest of the gang. I just saw them dodge into Jubilee Gardens. Run for it!' she hissed and started to sprint. 'Now!'

They were down onto the cycleway that ran alongside the canal, and away, making the most of their few seconds' advantage.

Feet connected with the path behind and yelling started up in the high wooded bank above them. The Riley twins and Malc Conway were crashing through the undergrowth, trying to head them off, shouting and whooping like extras in a movie.

The path took the lazy curve of the canal and all the time Greg Simpson was steadily whittling down the space between them. Alex fought to regulate her breathing and ignore the first grabbing pains of a stitch. They were running as fast as they could but he would be going faster. He wasn't scared, he was in control, and he was the best runner in the school. He'd done cross-country for the county. Soon he'd be close enough to call the others down like a pack of dogs on them.

Lauren was well ahead, nearly out of sight round the next bend. She ran with an easy, practised fluidity. A kind of hope leapt up in Alex as she realized that the other girl's greater height and longer legs could probably get her away.

'You go on,' she gasped, as Lauren dropped back.

'Leave the path at the next bridge.' She doubled over, hands on thighs, fighting for breath. 'There'll be kids from Radley School crossing. Get in amongst them and stay with them till you get to the shops. You'll be safe then.'

There was a shout from above as Malc reported that they had stopped. They glanced up to see him starting a leaping diagonal descent, the twins right behind him. Greg was shouting back, his pounding steps close now. They were moving in.

'Go on!' Alex said with new urgency. 'You can get away, you run faster than me!'

'No,' Lauren said simply.

'You must!' Alex was desperate now, almost crying. 'If they catch us, they'll kill us.'

'Better not catch us then. Come on!' Lauren said and grabbed her hand. 'Not far now, you'll see.'

Lauren started off again and Alex dredged up the last of her strength to follow. Her legs felt like rubber and her chest was on fire. Running was hopeless. They'd never make it to the bridge. They might as well turn and face what was coming.

'Just up here. You can make it, Alex!' Lauren shouted over her shoulder.

As they rounded the corner, she stopped so suddenly Alex cannoned into her.

'Look!' she said, pointing in front of her.

Alex wiped the sweat and hair out of her eyes, wondering what they were supposed to be looking at.

'Barges!' Lauren cried and leapt on to the nearest one, dragging Alex after her.

Two or three barges were lined up, waiting to go through the lock up ahead. A middle-aged man in shorts and a beany hat, a T-shirt clinging tight to his rolls of fat, stood at the front of the one they had jumped. He turned, startled by the movement of the boat.

'Hey!' he yelled and started to make his way down the narrow space along the side of the cabin. 'What do you think you are doing? Muriel!' he shouted, banging on the roof. 'We've got boarders.'

The little door opened and a woman in pink shorts and a halter top came out. Pale skin bulged from under short sleeves as she stared at them, arms folded tightly.

'Hi,' Lauren started before she could open her mouth. 'I'm Lauren. I'm from Australia,' she said by way of explanation. Her accent was getting noticeably thicker and her smile more dazzling. 'I ran all the way when I saw you down here. I hope you don't mind but I just had to get a look at your boat. I've heard so much about them, but I've never seen one close to – only pictures.'

'They're called long boats,' the man said, still suspicious.

'Or narrow boats,' his wife added stiffly.

'Is that right?' Lauren's grin widened. 'Fascinating.'

'Your friend,' the man indicated Alex, 'is she from Australia too?'

'Oh, no,' Lauren shook her head, 'she's from around here, aren't you, Alex?'

Alex nodded. She was still out of breath but she managed a smile and some of the fear inside her began to evaporate.

Greg Simpson and his gang came storming round

the corner, greedy for the kill. They stopped when they saw Alex and Lauren up on the narrow boat and stood on the towpath, staring at them. Greg's fists curled and uncurled in silent rage, the others looked at him, mouths half open, brows furrowing in confusion.

'They're friends of yours too?' The man eyed the boys with undisguised distrust.

'What?' Lauren turned towards them. 'Never seen them before in my life. Have you, Alex?'

Alex shook her head. The man's hostile glare became positively ferocious and the gang began to melt away, retracing their steps, as Lauren started to ask lots of interested questions about long boats.

'It's really quite big inside.' The woman pushed the little door open so they could take a look. 'I've got a brother living in Adelaide,' she said to Lauren as they peered in. 'What part of Australia are you from?'

'Perth,' Lauren replied.

The boat in front was starting to manoeuvre its way into the lock.

'Come on, Muriel,' the man shouted, making his way as fast as he could along the side of the boat. 'We're on the move. Get to the tiller quick. Don't just stand there gossiping.'

He took up his former position at the front.

'Do you two want to lend a hand?' he called.

'Yes, OK. What do we do?' Lauren shouted back.

They helped them get through the lock, hopping on and off, turning this and that. It was fun and for a few minutes Alex forgot all about Greg Simpson.

At the bridge, they jumped off and climbed up to

the road. They crossed over and leaned out waving the couple goodbye from the parapet.

They joined the crowds streaming across from Radley Comprehensive. Alex found Helen and introduced her to Lauren. There was no sign of the gang so they were safe. For the moment.

All the way back, Lauren practically danced along, entertaining Helen with the story of their triumph. Alex hardly said anything. Lauren's jumping onto the boat and her performance there, the sudden charm and brilliant smile, had stunned her into silence. It had been so unexpected. Nothing she knew about the other girl had prepared her for it. Alex herself would rather have faced Greg Simpson than get onto a strange boat like that, and been torn limb from limb and all the pieces thrown into the canal to feed the fishes.

'Phew!' Helen said after they waved goodbye to Lauren at the end of her road. 'She's not at all like you said. Are you sure you've got her right, Alex?'

Chapter 14

The next day, after school, Alex was standing in the playground, minding her own business, when Sandi and Andrea came up to her.

'We've come to tell you something,' Sandi said.

'Yeah,' Andrea joined in, 'about your friend.'

Alex confronted them, arms folded, silent.

'She's a liar and a thief,' Sandi continued.

'It's right,' Andrea insisted, on cue. 'She stole Sandi's sunglasses!'

'Oh, yeah?' Alex curled her lip in contempt. 'How do you know?'

'We've got proof,' Andrea crowed. 'I seen her!'

'And we're going to Quaid about it. If you're friends with her – people'll think you're the same, won't they? She's going to get you into trouble, Alex.'

'Yeah, get you into trouble, Alex,' Andrea chimed in like a little echo.

'Thanks for the warning,' Alex said sarcastically, 'but I'll make my own mind up about my friends. Anyway' – she regarded them both for a moment – 'maybe I've got something to tell you . . .'

'What about?' Sandi demanded.

'About Greg.'

'Like what?'

'Oh, that he asked Lauren out and she told him to get lost.'

'That's crap,' Andrea shouted. 'He can't stand her!'

'That's not what I heard . . .' Alex smiled. Sandi's face was turning as pink as her dress. 'Someone told me—'

'It's a lie!' Andrea interrupted. 'Who'd fancy her?'

Greg for one, and Sandi knows it, Alex thought, as the blonde girl shouted, 'Shut up, Andrea!'

'Ask him yourself,' Alex said, but suddenly her confidence was draining away. 'Here he comes.'

She knew they wouldn't, but neither would she. Sandi and Andi were no contest, Alex was not in the least bit scared of them, but Greg was a different matter altogether. She instinctively knew that taunting him with something like that would be about as sensible as teasing a Rottweiler.

'You told her?'

The two girls nodded.

'Told me what?' Alex asked innocently.

'Keep away from her, Lewis.' Greg Simpson was standing right in front of her now. He took her loosely by the shoulders. 'This is the last time. And we're not warning you, we're telling you.'

His eyes were an odd grey-brown, hard as polished stone: blank and expressionless, like there was no one home. His grip tightened until his thumbs felt like two steel rods biting into the soft flesh below her collar-bones. All the time he stared down at her, absolutely confident of his ability to terrify.

'You listen. Last night was meant for her, not you. But you hang round with her any more, you'll get what's coming too. And that's a promise. All right?' he said, pushing her away finally with the palms of his hands. 'You understand?'

With a flick of his head he summoned the rest of the gang and they left her, Sandi and Andrea tagging along at their heels.

'What did they want?' Lauren said as she came up with Caroline.

'The usual.' Alex stared after them. 'What do you think?'

She watched them swagger away. They meant what they said. Something had to be done, and quickly, or it would go on and on, just like it had with Bailey.

'Did he really ask you out?' Alex asked, massaging her shoulder.

'Yeah . . .' Lauren mumbled, colour washing her cheeks.

'And did you really tell him to—'

'Yeah, but who wouldn't?'

'What did you say, exactly?'

Lauren fixed her piercingly clear grey eyes on Alex. 'I said I'd rather go out with a rabid dog than you.'

Alex grinned, regarding the other girl with open admiration. 'Not much of a choice, really.'

'No.' Lauren laughed. 'Come on, let's go.'

'You know Sandi's sunglasses?' Alex remarked as they went out of the gates. 'Can you bring them in tomorrow? I think I've got an idea. Why don't you come for tea at my house and I can explain it to you.'

The next morning Alex joined Lauren on the way into school. They delivered Caroline safely to the Junior Annexe but when they turned to go back to their own playground, the Bridge Boys were waiting by the wall, along with Sandi and Andrea.

'Where do you think you're going?' Greg Simpson snarled.

'Registration,' Alex replied coolly.

'Well, you ain't. We've got business.'

The rest crowded round so from the outside they would look like any other playground huddle.

'Oh, yeah. What?' Alex said.

'Sandi's sunglasses. Didn't you tell her?' Greg turned to Lauren, laughing softly. 'We know you took them.'

'I don't know what you're talking about,' Lauren countered. 'What would I want with her cheap tacky sunglasses?'

Lauren concentrated on keeping her nerve and staring them out. But still her hand went to her side. The sunglasses felt heavy in her pocket. Insecure, like they could spill out of their own accord.

'Don't bother trying to deny it,' Greg sneered. 'You were seen.'

'Yeah,' Andrea popped up by his side. 'By me. And I seen you wearing 'em at the weekend,' she added for good measure.

'You can't have! I—' Lauren answered, and then stopped, aware that what she was about to say could give her away.

'See! See!' Andrea crowed. 'She has got 'em. That's proof!'

'Doesn't prove anything, Andrea,' Alex said quickly. 'She can't be seen wearing something she doesn't have, can she?'

'Yes, but—' Andrea started.

'Shut it, Andi,' Sandi snapped. 'We know you got them.' She pointed at Lauren. 'And don't think you can get out of it by giving them back.'

'No.' Greg folded his arms, grinning. 'She don't want to risk catching anything off your greasy zitty face.' They all sniggered. 'So she wants paying for 'em. Ain't that right, Sand?'

'Yeah. I want compensation.'

'So' – Greg spat on the ground and rubbed in the spittle as though he was considering – 'we reckon a tenner ought to do it. What do you say? A fiver each.'

Alex let out a gasp at the amount. Lauren stared at them speechless.

'And we want it by tomorrow,' Greg went on. 'And it's a pound each day you don't pay. Or else.'

'Or else what?' Alex managed to say.

'Or else,' Greg's thin grin widened, 'you both get a real battering.' He was right in Alex's face now. She could smell his sour breath. 'Remember what happened to Bailey? And he didn't have a little sister to worry about, did he?' He backed away and pointed a finger like a gun at her. 'Tomorrow. Same place. And you better have it ready.'

'It'll be all right, you'll see. Calm down,' Alex said as they watched them walking away.

'I don't know, Alex. I mean, I've got them right here in my jacket. What if they go to Quaid right now . . .'

'They won't. It's going to be OK, don't worry.' Alex smiled reassuringly. 'It's a good plan. Trust me.'

Lauren regarded Alex from under eyebrows drawn together in one black bar. All her old suspicion came flooding back.

'Why should I?'

'Because I'm your friend,' Alex said simply. 'And I'm the only one you've got. Give me the glasses if you're worried.' She held out her hand.

'Are you sure?' Lauren asked as she fumbled them out of her pocket.

'Sure, I'm sure. Hurry up, Quaid's coming. It's going to work, Lauren. Really.'

'You go in to class,' Alex said as they entered the deserted cloakroom.

'What?'

'You heard. Just go. There's no point in both of us getting caught. I'll only be a minute or two.'

Lauren stared at Alex for a moment, undecided. 'Oh, all right,' she said, turning to leave. Then she smiled. 'I guess I do trust you.'

'Good.' Alex smiled back. 'Now go.'

Alex was last in to the classroom. As she sat down at her table, Josie ostentatiously moved away. She herded all her things up to the other end of the desk with a sweep of her hand.

'You two better keep an eye on your stuff, and all,' she muttered to the boys opposite. 'Things get taken round here if you don't watch out.'

Class 7Q had PE first lesson. They drifted back from the field, late as usual, and jostled about getting changed back into their everyday clothes; boys in the classroom, girls in the cloakroom. Just as the bell

91

was about to go a cry went up from the far corner pegs.

'Ms Quaid!' Alex Lewis hopped up, one foot bare on the cold floor. 'I've lost one of my socks.'

Everyone groaned. It could be anywhere, a thorough search could take all break-time.

'Are you sure?' Ms Quaid said, pushing her short red hair off her face. 'Have you had a proper look?'

'Yes, Ms Quaid. I've looked everywhere.' Alex peered up at her in distress. 'They're new, Miss. My mum'll kill me if I've lost one and I can't go round all day with a bare foot.'

'Well,' Ms Quaid frowned down at her, 'why don't you wear your PE socks?'

Alex wailed in protest.

'They're all wet and soggy.' She looked round. 'Maybe someone's put it in their bag by mistake. Can't we have a quick look?'

'Oh, all right.' Ms Quaid sighed with impatience, the possibility of break-time coffee was disappearing fast. 'OK, everyone. Open your bags.'

'What does it look like, Alex?' she asked as Alex rummaged through Melanie's bag.

'Like this.' Alex held up a lone white slouch sock and moved on to Andrea. 'Marks and Spencers.' She delved under Andrea's pumps pulling out a tangle of assorted socks and sweaty old T-shirts. 'Maybe this is it.' She held up a sock. 'Oh, no, sorry. Hey, what's that?' Something black and pink fell from the unfurled sock and clattered across the floor. Alex bent to retrieve them. 'Aren't these Sandi's sunglasses, Ms Quaid? The ones she thought she'd lost?'

Andrea's expression changed from impatient

resentment to horrified disbelief. Her eyes widened behind her own thick lenses and her thin lips pulled back from her prominent front teeth in something between a grimace and a nervous grin.

'Sandi? Are these yours?' Ms Quaid held up the glasses. 'How did they get there? Andrea? What do you know about this?'

Sandi nodded, slitted eyes staring past the teacher, fixed on Andrea. The bell went and, as Ms Quaid turned to dismiss the class, Sandi mouthed: 'You're dead, Andrea Bowman!'

Ms Quaid, carrying the sunglasses, shepherded the two girls back to the classroom and everyone headed out for break. Alex limped off to get her sock from where she'd hidden it and Lauren came over to join her.

'Told you.' Alex grinned as she pulled on her sock. 'Worked like a dream, didn't it?'

'Yeah.' Lauren grinned back. 'What made you pick on her?'

'I know how they operate. If Andrea's their witness, it would have been her job to plant them. Also,' Alex said, picking up her trainers, 'she's been trying them on a lot, putting them over her own glasses or prancing round in them blind as a bat. She's always messing with Sandi's things. That gave me an idea. They might think she took them herself. None of them like her.'

'I thought, you know, Sandi 'n Andi – best friends,' Lauren said.

'Not really – that's what Andrea thinks, but Sandi doesn't like anybody much, apart from Sandi. She lets Andrea hang round because she likes the way she sucks up to her. They'll probably start on her next.' Alex gave a mirthless laugh. 'I wouldn't like to be Andrea.'

'But what if they don't think it's her – what if they think it's us?'

'Doesn't matter. They'll still blame Andrea for letting them down and they can't use the sunglasses to blackmail you any more, can they?'

'No,' Lauren smiled. 'Good thinking, Alex!'

'Yeah, well,' Alex finished tying her laces, 'don't get too excited. It isn't over yet. Greg Simpson doesn't give a toss about Andrea or the sunglasses. He's doing it because he enjoys making people miserable and, if he thinks he can make us give him money, this won't stop him. He won't like what's just happened. Whatever they do next, we'd better be ready. I wish David was here,' she said as she stood up, 'at least we'd have one ally.'

Chapter 15

The next day Alex was on full alert, jumping at sudden movements and loud sounds, waiting for another attack. But nothing dramatic happened. In some ways Alex wished it had. What could hurt more than the sly digs and insults, left to fester like sores, and the growing awareness that people she'd known since Nursery were not even speaking to her?

Not one of them, not a single one of them, was prepared to stand up to Greg and his gang. She bit her lip, fighting back tears, wishing David was here. He'd sure picked a great time to go on holiday. David was her friend and he wasn't scared of Simpson. He'd have stood by her, but he wouldn't be back in school until at least Monday. When they started on at her this lunch-time, even Neil, Dave's best mate, had turned away with a funny little smile and a what-can-I-do shrug.

She dragged home that Thursday afternoon, hardly aware of the route she took. She was tired of thinking about the same thing, it was like being in a game they couldn't win, every move they made was blocked. Her mind was still scurrying about like a frantic rat looking for ways out, and it was some time before she realized there was someone behind her. Someone on a bike who kept riding up and stopping, again and again. Finally he wheeled round in front, and there he was on a BMX, his long legs jacked right up, Greg Simpson.

'Didn't think anyone rode those any more,' Alex said, looking round. He appeared to be on his own but she kept on walking.

'I do,' he replied, standing up and spinning the bike on its back wheel. He fell in beside her. 'I want to talk to you.'

'Go on, then. I'm not stopping you.'

'The sunglasses. I told Sandi that stupid slag Andrea would cock it up.' He shook his head. 'Nice touch, Alex.' He laid his hand, lumpy and rough in its BMX glove, on her bare arm. 'But don't get the wrong idea that it, like, lets you off or anything.'

She swung round to confront him.

'What do you mean?'

'You still have to pay. Tell your mate and all. Tenner tomorrow, without fail. Or . . .'

'Or what?'

'Or next time it's more than her picture gets slashed. That sister of hers' – he grimaced in exaggerated disgust – 'she ain't exactly pretty as it is – all that long straggly hair . . .'

'Can't tomorrow,' Alex said, trying to keep her voice even.

'Oh!' His stony eyes narrowed to slits and he massaged his jaw with his dirty fraying glove. 'Why's that?'

'Er, won't be at school. Dental appointment.'

He laughed and mounted his bike, holding it steady with his knees.

'Cancel it.' He grinned at her, lips peeled back to show narrow lines of teeth. 'Be there – with the money. Or', he pulled up the glove, flexing his fingers, 'little Caroline's going to get a haircut. And that's just for starters. Be seeing you, Alex.'

He skidded away, riding the bike high and arrogant, doing trick turns and wheelies, before he disappeared. Alex sat on a nearby wall. She hadn't got far to go but suddenly she didn't feel too good, her legs were shaking. The game was going to a different level. She leaned forward, hands on her knees. What he'd said made her sick to her stomach. Imagine feeling this way every single day, for weeks, months, years even. This is what it must have been like for Michael Bailey. She swallowed hard as her mouth filled with saliva, her heart beating hollow and heavy inside her.

She rubbed her arms. They were covered in goosebumps. The weather had turned cold again and a spiteful gusting wind was tearing at the last of the blossom, scattering it over her like confetti. She'd seen Bailey once. She'd been passing in the car with her mum, and he'd been sitting on a wall, all hunched over, just like she was now.

Her mind jumped onto another track. That's why it had happened, that day two years ago in March, Bailey's last. He'd told them he wouldn't pay any more. He'd stopped paying.

Chapter 16

They watched him all the time, the Game was never far from the surface. Sometimes they watched idly, looking up briefly from other distractions, just to let him know they were there. But today, Michael Bailey sensed a rippling excitement passing from one to another. In the way a pack of dogs might ready itself for the hunt, there was an eagerness, a heightening of anticipation.

They started their campaign as soon as he got to school, calling him names, filling his desk with unspeakable things, saying things about his mother; but that was just routine stuff.

He said that he'd spilt something in his desk and stayed in at break, salvaging what he could, trying not to bring what he was doing to the notice of Mrs Harris. He had to go to the big bin outside, but returned to the classroom unscathed. Mrs Harris was sitting at her desk marking books and drinking her coffee. She smiled at him as he came in and murmured something. He almost managed to smile back. He felt safe with her. He sat at his desk, gingerly examining his feelings as a doctor might probe a deep injury for signs of healing. Perhaps he was wrong about it starting again, perhaps it would stop now he had stood up to them.

It wasn't sudden bravery that had made him tell

them he wasn't going to pay any more. It was just a different sort of fear. Del and the Bridge Boys had got too greedy, demanding more and more for their 'protection'. He'd told them there was no way he could get that much money, not every week, but Del had just laughed and told him to steal it. Michael couldn't do that. Mum and Dad had already started to notice small sums of money going missing and they suspected him already, at least Dad did. He'd heard them talking one night when they thought he was in bed, his father's voice deep and serious, outlining his suspicions, his mother defending him blindly, 'Our Michael wouldn't do that, Frank,' almost in tears. If it went on, they'd find out and never, never trust him, even they would start to hate him.

He had considered, as he stood in the dimly lit hall listening, going in to them and confessing, telling them why he was taking money, what was happening to him. But that was unthinkable. He had been silent too long and it would upset his mother terribly. Anything that hurt him seemed to wound her much more deeply. The only way to protect her was to make sure she never knew anything about it. And the only way to do that was to stop paying the money and take what was coming. It was not a matter of choice, or courage, at all.

He thought they might be planning to get him at lunch-time but nothing happened on the way to the dining hall. Michael Bailey had school dinners and always ate alone. He collected his tray and allowed the cook to fill his plate. She asked him what he wanted but he didn't answer so she put on a bit of everything. She watched him shuffle away. He was a strange one, that one. She wondered why he always had his bag slung across him like that, none of the other kids did. She didn't know what would happen if he put it down anywhere, even for a second.

She nodded across to her friend, Ellen Brody, on duty the other side of the counter. They'd talked about Michael Bailey and the tricks the others played on him. Ellen had even gone to the Head about it, but all he'd said was that they were aware of the situation and they were monitoring it, like he wasn't too keen on being told how to do his job by dinner ladies. Ellen tried to keep an eye on Michael herself, but it wasn't easy. There was always something going on. As she said, in her job you needed eyes in the back of your head, not to mention other parts of your anatomy.

He found a place on a table of younger pupils. They automatically moved to avoid him but at least they didn't lean over to spit in his food, or pour on water, or salt, chanting: 'Eat, piggy, eat.'

Michael Bailey didn't eat a great deal. He never did, despite what they said about him being a pig. He wasn't even fat, just a bit plumpish. He never ate much at school. Even when none of them were close to him the food still seemed contaminated.

He paced the playground in a set pattern, like an animal paces its enclosure after long years of confinement. He felt the tension knotting and knotting like a ball of rope inside him. None of them came near him, but he sensed the signals zinging between them. It was going to happen, it was just a matter of time. He wished it would happen right now. The waiting was the most terrible bit. It was better to know. Why didn't they get on with it? But they knew that, of course they did. The waiting, the stalking, was part of the Game.

The bell went for afternoon school and still nothing had occurred. He did not feel relief this time, just a lurch in the stomach, like seasickness. Nothing could be worse than this, he thought. Nothing. Sometimes he wished they would just kill him outright and get it over with.

They were waiting until after school. Michael worked through the afternoon on his part of a huge wall-frieze of the ages of the earth. Up until now he had enjoyed doing this. It was interesting and sometimes he could lose himself in what he was doing. It was somewhere they couldn't get to him.

But today he could not concentrate. The wind moaned round the classroom, periodically gathering itself and hurling sleet like bursts of shot at the window. Mrs Harris had turned the thermostat up but he felt chilled in the classroom's fuggy heat. By the window the cold seeped through the glass. Freezing air searched out all the little gaps in the swollen cracked frames, sometimes lifting the paper on his desk. Condensation stopped him from seeing out. It dribbled and ran, dripping onto the floor like a distillation of the hate forming around him.

Mrs Harris turned on the lights early and they watched him from the other side of the bright classroom, nudging and grinning. What was going to happen spread round, a sinister whispered under-current to the loud surface chatter and conversation.

At the centre of it all sat Greg Simpson, checking

off who was in and who was out. The few chosen to be directly involved, talked loud and swaggered around, glowing from his attention. They'd better not let him down. Bailey had been an easy and useful source of income. Del had not been pleased when Greg told him Bailey wouldn't pay any more. He'd laid into him like it was his fault. Greg shifted in his seat, easing his side and the bruising in his back, just above the kidneys. Del didn't leave marks but he could hurt you badly.

Sandi had sulked at first when he'd told her Del said only boys allowed, but she and Andrea would come through with a cover story if there was any trouble. There'd better not be any trouble. Greg's older brother had made it pretty clear what would happen if things went wrong. You had to hand it to Del, though, he was good. He only had to stamp on the ground now and Bailey was legging it off with all his flab jiggling about. Greg winced as he laughed to himself.

His lazy predatory gaze sharpened as he focused on the figure by the window. Bailey was such a fat little slug. If anyone deserved a good kicking, he did. Everything about him was asking for it and tonight he was going to get it. Lately, Bailey had been getting far too cosy, thinking he could avoid them, hiding behind Harris, thinking he could blank them out. Time he was taught a proper lesson. Greg wasn't going to take any more beatings on his account.

Greg Simpson settled back in his chair. It was going to be OK. They were bound to get away with it. Bailey would pay, he could almost hear those pound coins chinking, and he wouldn't tell either, because he knew the next time would be that much worse. None of the others would say anything. That was what was really good about it. He'd got them all like that, he screwed his thumb into the side of the desk. Bailey had absolutely no friends. Even people like Alex Lewis and David Morris hated Bailey almost as much as he did.

Chapter 17

'Alex? What are you doing? Get in.'

Alex looked round, startled. A car door was opening and her mother's face was hanging over the passenger seat. She dumped a bag of shopping on the floor, to make room for her daughter, and Alex got in.

She mumbled something about not feeling very well and her mother didn't question her further; but when they were in the house, she gently pushed her daughter's curly hair back so she could see her face and said quietly, 'Let's have a cup of tea, shall we? And then maybe we can talk about it.'

Alex didn't say a word as the kettle roared to a boil and clicked itself off. Steam billowed as her mother filled the teapot.

'Now then,' her mother said, bringing the tea over to the table, 'what's the matter? Is it something that's happened at school?'

'No,' Alex said quickly.

'Are you sure?' her mother asked as she opened a packet of biscuits.

'Yes, of course. It's nothing, Mum, honest. It's . . .' Alex took her mug and drank some scalding tea. 'Like I said, I just felt funny.'

'I don't mean that, Alex.' Her mother looked at her over the rim of her cup. 'There's something wrong, something else, isn't there? And I think it's time we talked.' She put her cup down, brushing away her daughter's protests. 'There's no point in denying it, Alex. This came this morning.' She held up an envelope with the school's crest on it. 'And Helen's already spoken to me about it.' She put a finger to her lips to hush Alex's angry reaction. 'Helen was worried and she was right to tell me. She cares about you. We all do. And you haven't been yourself lately, even Dad noticed there was something the matter.'

Her mother listened quietly, sipping her tea, as Alex reluctantly told her what it was all about. It was muttered and halting, the incidents coming in random order, but eventually the story covered everything, from the first time Alex noticed them picking on Lauren to this last awful week, when everything had got much worse and Alex had been included.

By the time she had finished, her tea was cold. Her mother threw it away and poured her another.

'I'm glad you've told me,' she said, putting her arms around her daughter and hugging her. 'Now, we better get cracking and do something about it, hadn't we?' She gave Alex's shoulder a quick squeeze and released her. 'Have you got Lauren's number? I think I ought to phone her mother.'

'You can't, Mum.' Alex looked up, stricken. 'She'll kill me if she thinks I've told anyone – especially you.'

Her mother frowned down at her, puzzled. 'Who will?'

'Lauren!'

'Don't be silly, Alex. Of course she won't. Give me the number.'

Alex handed it over, knowing she didn't have any

choice. Her mother took it and went into the hall. A phone call like that could punch right through their fragile friendship, but there was no point in arguing or trying to tell her. That was the trouble with adults. They could only understand so far. In Lauren's world there were things you didn't do and Alex had just broken the most important rule. The one that said: Don't go talking about it. Whatever happens.

Her mother came back, brisk and efficient.

'Mrs Price has had a letter, too. She was just going to phone me about it. They're coming over. Six o'clock.' She reached down and ruffled her daughter's hair. 'We'll soon have it sorted out, Alex, don't you worry.'

Alex rested her head on the table. What was she going to do? She felt sick again. Weak and stupid. She should never have told. Now she had, how would she ever be able to face Lauren?

Chapter 18

It was clear, right from the start, that Lauren was not going to make it easy.

Mrs Price sat on the edge of a chair in the living room, still in her coat, pushing her thick dark hair back into its untidy plait, as she listened to a summary of what had been happening to her daughter. Her large eyes darkened with shock and concern as the full extent of the bullying was revealed and her pretty face became tense with alarm and worry.

Lauren had shot one furious glaring look at Alex when they first came into the house. Now she sat next to Caroline on the couch, staring at her hands, apparently impassive.

'Lauren?' Mrs Price turned to face her daughter. 'Is this true? My God,' she said, shaking her head, 'I thought there was something, but I thought it was just settling in. I had no idea . . . You poor kid.' She reached for her daughter's hand. 'Why didn't you tell me?'

Lauren snatched her hand away and folded her arms tightly. 'It's not true,' she said, eventually. 'She's making it all up. Making a mountain out of a molehill.'

Alex stared in amazement, she could hardly keep her mouth from dropping open.

'Why would I do that?' she managed to ask at last,

uncomfortably aware that they were all looking at her.

'How should I know?' Lauren snarled. 'Because you're scared. Because it's you it's happening to. To gain attention. Don't ask me.' She shrugged. 'I'm not a psychiatrist.'

Alex shook her head slowly, unable to believe what she was hearing. 'It's not ... I wouldn't ...' she started and then she stopped. She looked round helpless, not knowing what to say. Lauren's words had brought her to the verge of tears.

'Hey!' Helen said from the door where she'd been listening. 'Alex wouldn't lie, not about a thing like that!'

'How would you know?' Lauren sneered up at her. 'You're not exactly close, are you? You're a real bitch to her most of the time, she told me.'

Helen's whole body tensed but her angry reply was cut off by a warning look from her mother.

'Lauren ...' Mrs Price started but whatever she was going to say was cut short.

'It's all your fault!' Lauren shouted across the room at her mother. 'Yours and Dad's. It wouldn't have happened if we hadn't come here. It was his idea to come and you gave in. Both of you said how great it was going to be, especially Dad. And now we're here, we never even see him. He's always away, or late, or out someplace and when he is there all you ever do is row and go on at each other. I hate it. I want to go back, back home to Australia. And so do you, and if you say you don't, you're – you're a hypocrite!'

Lauren sat back into the settee, white-faced, arms

folded. She knew that she had gone way too far, but she hadn't been able to stop herself, the resentment and anger that had been gathering for months had all come raging out of her. She was appalled at herself, how could she do that? To Mum especially. Tears pricked at the back of her nose, but she sniffed them back and stared around, regarding them all with defiance.

No one said anything. Lauren's gaze was fixed on her mother but Mrs Price just sat staring down, twisting her wedding ring round and round.

'You've been so kind,' she said eventually, addressing Mrs Lewis, 'and' – she shrugged in despair – 'I don't know what's got into Lauren, she's not usually this ... unpleasant.' She looked away from her daughter and tried to smile but her eyes were filling with tears and her lips trembling. 'We've taken up enough of your time,' she said suddenly, reaching for her bag. 'We'd better be going.'

'Don't go yet,' Alex's mother said. 'You're upset. I know' – she smiled – 'would you like a glass of wine? I've got a bottle in the fridge and John's away at the moment, so I need an excuse to open it. Go on. Say you'll stay and help me drink it.'

'No, no really ...' Mrs Price started to get up but Alex's mother gently put a hand on her arm to restrain her.

'You must. I insist. One glass won't hurt. You've still got your coat on. Here, let me take it.' She turned to her daughters, throwing them Mrs Price's jacket. 'Here, Alex, hang this up and then take Lauren up to your room. And Helen, you look after Caroline, will you?'

Alex hung the coat on the bannister and followed Lauren up the stairs, away from the distant sound of a cork being pulled and adult voices introducing themselves and getting to know each other. Thanks, Mum, she thought to herself. The mood Lauren was in she might as well have sent her off to entertain a pit-bull terrier.

'What did you have to go and tell for? You little dobber,' Lauren accused as soon as they were in the room.

'I – I had to. Mum made me,' Alex replied, trying to defend herself. 'Anyway, they both had the letters.'

'So what?' Lauren glared at her. 'You didn't have to go and tell them the whole story, did you?'

'What was I supposed to do . . .'

'You could have thought of something. "Mum made me",' Lauren said, mocking Alex's accent. 'That's really pathetic!'

'Oh? And what were you going to do about it!' Alex hit back, infuriated. 'Sit around sulking and sneering, I suppose. Hiding behind me. Waiting for me to sort it all out for you!'

Lauren's grey slanting eyes narrowed as Alex's words stung home.

'What did you say?' she demanded, her voice cold and hard as she took hold of the front of Alex's shirt.

'Stop it!' Helen came between them, forcing them apart. 'Pack it in both of you!'

Helen held them at arms' length. She pushed Alex on to the bed, keeping hold of Lauren.

'You shouldn't be fighting each other,' she said.

'She lied downstairs,' Alex shouted. 'And upset everyone!'

Lauren tried to wriggle out of Helen's grip. 'She shouldn't have told!'

'Why not?' Helen asked, addressing Lauren.

'Because . . .' Lauren exploded and then tailed off, at a loss. 'Because you don't tell. And there was no need. I can handle it myself.'

'Can you?' Helen looked sceptical. 'You sure about that?'

'Sure.' Lauren squared her shoulders and balled her fists. 'No worries.'

Helen let go of Lauren and folded her arms. 'You haven't done too well so far, have you?' she said thoughtfully. 'And what about Caroline? Can you protect her?'

'Yeah,' Lauren said, less certain now. 'Sure I can.'

'Well, you can't. Not on your own,' Helen said, kicking a pile of cushions together and sitting down. 'It was me who told Mum, to start with, anyway. Are you going to fight me too?' She paused for a moment. 'Look, Lauren, it's got to be stopped. Now. Or it'll just go on and on.' She looked over at Alex. 'Have you told her about Bailey?'

'Some,' Alex said, 'not all of it.'

'That kid who's supposed to be a ghost?' Lauren sneered. 'Sounds like a dork. I'm not like that.'

Helen shrugged and leaned back into the cushions.

'Tell her, Alex. Tell her what they did to Bailey.'

Alex sat up on the edge of the bed and cleared her throat. When she spoke her voice was so low they had to lean forward to hear her.

'OK,' she said, 'but it wasn't just Greg or Del, his older brother, or the Bridge Boys. You've got to understand that. In a way it was everyone, all of us.'

She closed her eyes, taking herself back for the second time in the space of a few hours to that day two years ago.

'It was March, and cold for the time of year, very cold. Mrs Harris, we were in Year Five then, made some crack about spring never coming. It was the same kind of thing as usual to start with, messing up his stuff, saying he stank, calling him names . . .'

'And you did it too?' Lauren interrupted. 'You joined in?'

'Yes. We all did. We were all part of it,' Alex said fiercely. 'I just told you. But that particular day was different. Every week Bailey had to pay the Bridge Boys money to leave him alone and – and he'd told them he wasn't paying any more. So we all knew that something serious was going to happen,' she said, picking up her story. 'But no one was prepared to do anything because nobody liked him.'

Chapter 19

Michael Bailey sat in his place after school, his last
hope fading with the footsteps disappearing down
the corridor. Maybe Mrs Harris thought she was
doing him a favour by keeping him back, maybe she
thought that by doing that she could protect him.
She didn't know that his only chance lay in the safety
of a crowd, safest of all amongst the mothers with
buggies who came to meet the younger pupils.

He got up, wooden and numb, mechanically fol-
lowing Mrs Harris's instructions. She didn't know
about, or underestimated, Greg Simpson's infinite
patience, in matters like this anyway. He might be
lazy and idle in the classroom, but in some things he
was capable of careful planning and great ingenuity.

The others staying behind were uneasy too,
because they knew what was going on and didn't
want to get involved. One by one they made their
escape, until only two were left: Alex Lewis and
Michael Bailey.

'Simpson's waiting for you, Bailey,' Alex hissed as
they put up the last bit of the display. 'You ought to
tell Harris about it.'

Michael handed her a drawing pin and shook his
head. He gave her a sick little smile but didn't say
anything. He couldn't explain, even if he'd wanted
to, how far it had gone with him. He couldn't tell

anyone, or ask their help, such a thing was impossible. He felt like a prisoner, shut up for so long he could not face the sun. Even with the bars gone and the doors wide open, the world contained no possibility of freedom.

Alex sighed with impatience, savagely pushing home the last drawing pin. That was the trouble with Bailey. He never did anything to help himself, never did anything to stop it. You had to stand up to bullies. Instead of that he waited around like a big soft punch bag, almost inviting people to hit him.

'OK, you two, I'll do the rest,' Mrs Harris said, dismissing them.

Alex watched Bailey collect his things and get ready to leave. He had that sick look on his face again but he still hadn't said anything. She wondered briefly if she ought to, and then just as swiftly dismissed the idea. It was best not to get involved. If he didn't want to tell the teacher, why should she?

The only way to deal with bullies was to stand up to them, she said to herself again as she followed him out. That's what she would do. If that was true why was she walking so slow? Why was she deliberately dawdling?

Alex stood in the corridor, guiltily picking at the corner of a tattered wall display. Then she turned and walked quickly and purposefully towards the cloakroom.

She couldn't hear anything. She stood for a moment thinking perhaps they had gone, perhaps she'd been wrong. Then a door banged hard, and running feet made her jump back and hide among the few remaining coats. When she came out, it was very quiet, you could even hear the taps dripping. She listened hard. There was another sound, a kind of whimpering. It didn't even sound human, more like an animal. She tracked it down to the Boys' toilets.

Alex hesitated. She had never been in there, not even for a dare, and she couldn't bring herself to go in now. She dashed off, telling herself she was looking for a teacher or a cleaner, someone authorized. Deep inside her she knew it was because she didn't want to see, didn't know how to help, whoever was making that noise.

She rounded a corner and crashed into Mr Derby. He wasn't Head then, just Deputy, but like now, even on freezing cold days, he always walked around without a jacket. It was exceptionally cold that day but he was in his shirt-sleeves. Alex remembered the expanse of white. He wore those metal band things to hitch the sleeves up. She could see the thick furry hair on his wrists and his gold watchstrap.

He steadied her and then held her away from him, smiling down. 'Who've we got here?'

'Alex Lewis, Mrs Harris's class,' she panted out automatically. 'You've got to come quickly, it's Michael Bailey . . .'

Something about the way she looked or the name she had spoken alerted him.

'Where?' he demanded.

'The cloakroom, Boys' toilets.'

He loped off, his tie flying behind him. When Alex caught up he was standing there with the door flung right open. She looked in under his arm. There was no one there. Bailey's bag lay on its side with the strap broken. His stuff was strewn all over the place, books torn and the pages scattered, the leaves lay sodden, wrinkled and plastered, his artwork weeping colours on to the wet and filthy floor.

Michael Bailey shuffled across the playground weeping uncontrollably, pulling his fouled coat around him and clutching at his trousers, trying to hold them up. He pushed in a shirt-tail and fumbled for the fastening. Everything he wore was filthy now, stinking. His new coat all torn and soaking, what was he going to tell his mother? The wind cut through his wet clothes and sleet froze the tears on his face. He'd never cried in front of them before, now he thought he would never stop.

They were waiting for him at the bridge. One lot waited at the far end. The others jumped out as soon as he had passed them, closing in behind him to cut off his escape.

'Bail-ey, Bail-ey, Bail-ey.'

The two syllables of his own name came in waves like a football chant, and then Greg Simpson, with his brother Del, stepped out of the crowd. They came towards him, crouching slightly, their grinning mouths identical as they beckoned for him to come towards them.

'Come on, come on, come on,' they said, like they were coaxing a dog.

Bailey looked from side to side. There was nowhere else to go. In spreading silence, he started to climb, and then he was over the parapet. He looked down. The edge of the bridge was tiny, so thin his black shoes stuck out over it. He could see the cars and lorries, far below, speeding between his feet. He stared, mesmerized by their movement. They looked small, unreal, like Scalectrix.

He leaned out like a diver, holding onto the rail behind him. The cold metal was quickly leaching all warmth and feeling. His hands no longer felt part of him. He didn't look round but another sound had joined the hypnotizing buzz and drone of the traffic.

It started with a single voice, slowly at first but it thickened and gathered pace as another voice joined, and then another, and another, until it was all of them, chanting a single word together:

'Jump, jump, jump, jump.'

It went on and on, faster and faster, until he couldn't be sure if it was inside or outside his head. Eventually his own voice joined in, convincing him of something he already knew. There was really no choice, it was the only way out for him. The one thing left that he could do.

'But he didn't, did he?' Caroline's small anguished voice brought Alex back to the present.

'What?' she asked thickly, as though she was waking up.

'He didn't jump, did he, Alex?'

'I thought you wanted him to be a ghost,' Lauren said quietly, but at her sister's look she apologized. 'All right, I'm sorry. Carry on with the story, Alex.'

Alex felt again the cold cutting through her sweat-shirt as she raced after Mr Derby towards the bridge, and heard the rhythmic chanting that came and went, booming on the wind. She saw the wide semi-circle of people crowding in towards its unseen centre. Mr Derby ran on but Alex checked her step. There must be half the school there. The line stretched from one end of the bridge to the other. In some places it was two or three deep. She could finally hear the word they were chanting over and over. It chilled deep inside her, turning her colder than any wind.

Mr Derby tore through to the centre, throwing people aside like dolls. His white arms stretched out to grasp the figure on the wrong side of the parapet. Michael Bailey half turned to the teacher and, at that moment, his foot slipped. The chanting lost its rhythm and started to falter. Bailey yelled once and his head and shoulders disappeared from view. The chanting stopped as suddenly as if someone had switched it off. In the silence Alex could hear the whine of the cars below them and the teacher's laboured breathing and muttered swearing. He held the boy by one arm and, although he was strong, he could not get him up by himself.

'Help me, some of you. I can't hold him much longer. Come and help me!'

None of them moved. The outer fringes were gliding backwards and in seconds that big crowd of people had melted away. Alex ran forward, joined by one or two others.

'. . . but we were all too short, we couldn't reach him.'

Alex shut her eyes and a familiar sick feeling swept through her like it did in her nightmares. In her dreams she saw over and over again the yawning space, the cars speeding below her, and Bailey falling, getting smaller and smaller, his arms and legs flailing out like he was swimming. Then there was the squealing of tyres, the crash and shatter of glass, the crunch of metal on metal as he disappeared, eaten by the edge of the bridge. But that was in her dreams. In real life it had happened differently.

'A man came along and he got hold of Michael on the other side, and him and Mr Derby together managed to pull him back,' she said, finishing the story abruptly.

'So he was all right?' one of them asked.

Alex did not reply. What was all right? She remembered, but would not describe, the look in his eyes as she had leant out and held out her hand to him. He had the most beautiful eyes she had ever seen, large and luminous, slaty-blue merging into purple, and they were full of the most terrible pleading. Not to be rescued. That was not what he wanted. He was pleading for them to let him go, let him fall. That expression, and the reason for it, would be with her as long as she lived.

No one spoke. They sat frozen, silenced by what she had told them.

Lauren moved first, looking up at Alex.

'That's really terrible,' she said quietly. 'That's a terrible story.'

'Yes,' Helen glanced at Alex and then replied for her. 'Pretty terrible.'

'But' – Lauren turned to her – 'didn't anything happen?'

'Like what?' Helen asked.

'I don't know. Didn't the school do anything about it?'

Helen shrugged. 'He climbed over the barrier. No one made him do it.'

'But they did!' Lauren shook her head impatiently. 'He climbed over to get away from them so it was their fault. They should have been . . .'

'What?' Helen asked, suddenly intense. 'Punished? Who were they going to punish, Lauren? Like Alex said, everybody was involved. You haven't been listening properly.'

'He climbed the barrier to get away from all of us,' Alex said and then she sighed. 'You can't punish everybody. You're right, though, the school should have done something . . .'

'But they didn't,' Helen said, finishing the sentence for her. 'Jenkins, the old Head, was absolutely hopeless, just swept it all under the carpet. What did he call it?'

'Schoolboy prank, he said it the next day, in Assembly,' Alex replied. 'It might have been different if Mr Derby had been Head then . . .'

'But he wasn't. So they just ignored it. Easier to do that than try and do something about it. Easier to pretend it never happened.'

'It would be different now, Helen,' Alex insisted.

Her older sister curled her lip. 'Maybe,' she said cynically. 'Mum'll be going up tomorrow, then we'll see. Meanwhile, watch your backs.' She turned to Lauren. 'You know what they're like now. What they do to people. Alex wasn't telling on you – she was just scared you were heading for the same treatment, that's all.'

Lauren looked at Helen, holding her hands up.

'All right, all right. You don't have to draw me a picture.' She turned to Alex and mumbled, 'I guess I owe you an apology.'

'That's OK.' Alex managed to smile back. 'Apology accepted.'

'You better apologize to your mum as well,' Helen said. 'You were pretty rude and said some pretty awful things to her.'

'Yeah, I know,' Lauren said and stood up to go downstairs.

Chapter 20

Everyone was up extra early the next morning, Alex's mum wanted them out of the house at least half an hour before the normal time. She went to get the car out as Alex and Helen put on their coats.

'Here,' Helen said. 'Take it then.'

'Oh.' Alex took a quick look and shook her head. 'I don't know, Helen.'

'What? You thought it was a great idea last night! It's easy. See?' Helen pointed out the different buttons. 'Press here and then again, here. It's all ready to go – I fixed it up. Only thing is' – she bit her lip – 'it may need batteries.'

'Where am I going to get batteries?' Alex demanded. 'I haven't got any money. Anyway, I've been thinking . . . there's no need to. Not if Mum's going in to see the Head.'

'Here,' Helen dug in her pocket for change, 'that should be enough. Do it, Alex. What if something goes wrong? It could be important. You never know – they might try to fob Mum off with stuff about playground rough and tumble and horseplay, like with Bailey. Or say it's half a dozen of one and six of the other. Your word against theirs.'

Alex shook her head. 'I don't think so . . .'

'It doesn't matter, one way or the other.' Helen sighed with impatience. 'What you need is evidence and with this you can prove it. Don't you see?'

'Oh, OK.' Alex took it from her reluctantly. 'But what about batteries?'

'Get Mum to stop at the garage . . .'

'She'll want to know why,' Alex objected. 'And it's Dad's. He'll go mad . . .'

'Nip out of school then, and go over to the newsagent's. You'll be there dead early, you've got plenty of time. Oh, and Alex,' Helen added as a blast from the horn summoned them to the car, 'keep any crap they give you – hate notes and that stuff. Anything you can use against them. Anything. Do you hear me?'

Alex nodded, slipping the little machine into her pocket as she closed the front door behind her.

'The Headmaster is out of school this morning, Mrs Lewis. Can I help you?'

Alex's mother and Mrs Bridges, the Deputy Head, were both trying to disguise a dislike for each other that went back to when Mrs Bridges had been Head of First School. Helen had been in her class, and she'd dismissed her lack of progress as inattentiveness, fussing about nothing. Then it was found that Helen had quite a serious hearing problem. Mrs Bridges had pegged the mother as overanxious and Janet Lewis had no intention of confiding her younger daughter's troubles to someone so insensitive.

'I'd prefer to speak to him personally, if you don't mind.'

'You better make an appointment, then. See the secretary about it.' She consulted the diary. 'He should be available this afternoon.'

'Could I see Ms Quaid? Alex's class teacher?'

Mrs Bridges looked at the diary again.

'Doctor's appointment,' she said with a thin smile. 'Not in either, I'm afraid.'

'I'll be back this afternoon,' Mrs Lewis said to Alex, who was waiting outside. 'Are you sure you'll be all right?'

'Yes, Mum. See you later.'

Alex watched her car pull out and then crossed over the road against the gathering flow of pupils and parents making their way to the school.

The newsagent's was crowded with people buying their morning papers and children agonizing over pick 'n' mix. Alex joined the queue, thinking about what was likely to happen that morning. Things were already going wrong. She fingered the machine Helen had given her, perhaps it was a good idea.

'You next?'

The assistant's voice cut into Alex's thoughts, hands clutching sweets and papers were waving at her from everywhere. She eyed Alex impatiently.

'Yes,' Alex said. 'Can I have a pack of batteries, please. No, not those. I want long-life ones.'

Alex checked her watch. Still plenty of time. She dodged into the service road behind the shops to put the batteries into the little tape recorder and then set off back to school. The service road acted as a short cut and she was nearly at the alleyway leading to the main road, when she heard a squashy tyre sound and the slight hiss and squeak of pulled-on brakes. It was a bike. Right behind her. The rider let her walk on, then rode up so close, the front wheel was almost nipping her legs, before letting her walk on again.

Alarms started going off in Alex's head as she continued on, pretending to ignore him. She should have stayed with the crowd. She looked to right and left, a brick wall one side and on the other nothing but bins and the backs of shops. The wheel was coming up again, almost touching the back of her knees. If I get caught here, she said to herself, I'm dead.

The next time he did it she stopped. The brakes screeched as he almost hit her. Rubber tore and skidded across the ground.

'All right!' she shouted. 'What the hell do you think you're doing?' Her fierce expression changed as she recognized the rider. 'Oh, it's you. Sorry, Dave.'

David Morris grinned at her sheepishly, his legs straddled wide over the bike sprawled out under him.

'I thought you were someone else.'

Alex stepped forward quickly to help him pull the bike up.

'Obviously,' Dave said as he removed his helmet. 'I thought you were going to do me over. I saw you dodge in here, I shouted at you but it was like I wasn't there. So I came up behind you. It was just a joke.'

'I know.' Alex smiled at him. 'I'm sorry. I just wasn't expecting you, that's all.'

He fell in beside her. Alex immediately lapsed into a silence.

'Hey, stop a minute.' David held her arm lightly. 'Is it something I've done?'

'What do you mean?'

'Don't I even get a "Hi, Dave. How was your holiday?" Did you remember to water the plants for me?'

'Oh, Dave. I'm sorry.'

He shrugged. 'That's all right. They're probably OK. Lucky we came back early.'

Alex didn't reply.

'Thanks for asking. Well,' Dave continued, 'it rained and it was freezing, Dad got a cold and spent the whole time moaning and Mum got hacked off with all of us.' He stopped. 'What's the matter, Alex?' he asked, suddenly serious.

'Nothing. I'll tell you later.'

'No.' He blocked her with his bike wheel. 'I want to know now.'

'OK' – Alex looked round – 'things have changed since you've been away, things have happened.'

'Like what?'

'Like, you know all that stuff last week with Lauren Price?'

David nodded.

'Well, they've started on me now. We're getting the Bailey treatment, the both of us.'

'Why?' David stared at her in amazement. 'I didn't even know you were friends with her.'

'That's one of the reasons.' Alex shrugged. 'Come on, the bell will be going in a minute. I'll tell you the rest as we're going along.'

David went off to park his bike and Alex was just on her way into the playground when a hand grabbed

126

her by the shoulder. She nearly jumped out of her skin.

Alex turned round slowly. It was Lauren.

'Come here a minute.' Alex pulled her behind a classroom wall. 'I've got something to show you.'

'I want to apologize, about last night,' Lauren was saying. 'Mum and me had a long talk when we got home – and I was wrong – about lots of things. And, and I want to say thanks – for putting me right. Mum made me see – I've been really pigheaded . . .'

'Don't say any more,' Alex said.

She looked round carefully to make sure no one was watching and then pulled something out of her pocket.

'Hang on.' She fiddled with the controls to get the right place. 'Listen to this.'

'. . . something to show you . . .'

There was a pause filled with the rustling of cloth and general noise. Then Lauren said:

'. . . I want to apologize . . .'

Lauren listened to her stumbling speech and stared at the miniature tape machine in astonishment.

'Hey!' she made a grab for it. 'Give it to me!'

Alex started to laugh. 'Not a chance! Lauren Price apologizes. It must be worth money.'

'Give it me! Or I'll . . .'

Alex whipped it out of her reach.

'Keep your hair on. I only did it to show you how it worked.'

'You better erase that!' Lauren glowered down at her.

'OK, OK.' Alex pressed a button. 'See? It's done.

We can use it to tape them – making threats and stuff. Then we can use the tape. Like evidence.'

'Cool idea.' Lauren raised one eyebrow in admiration.

Alex was tempted to claim it herself but then admitted Helen thought of it.

'Whoever,' Lauren said quietly. 'You better get it back in your pocket and turned on. It's showtime, Alex.'

The Bridge Boys were suddenly round them, cutting off their route back to the playground.

'You got it?' Greg Simpson demanded.

'Got what?' Alex replied.

'You know what. The money.'

The rest of the gang crowded in.

'No,' Alex said. 'I forgot how much it was.'

'Don't get funny with me, Lewis.' Simpson grabbed her arm.

'Ouch, let go. You're hurting me!' Alex screamed.

'Shut up, you stupid cow!' He gave her wrist another twist but he let go. 'Ten quid. A fiver each was what we agreed. And it's a pound each day you don't pay – starting now.'

'Or what?' Lauren asked.

'Or else' – Greg's thin grin widened – 'your sister gets it.' He jerked a thumb in Alex's direction. 'She knows. I want some of it lunch-time.'

'How are we supposed to get it by then?' Alex shouted.

'That's your problem. Go and rob a shop or something. See you later.'

Chapter 21

'What does he mean?' Lauren demanded after they had gone. 'About Caroline? What did he mean, Alex?'

'Nothing – just something he said – don't worry. Hold on.' Alex took the tape recorder out of her pocket. 'Let's see if it recorded.'

She pressed Rewind and they listened to the quick jumble of squeaky sound.

'Hey, it worked,' Lauren said excitedly. 'We can take this to Quaid and play it to her right now . . .'

'No, we can't.'

'Why not?' Lauren asked, mystified.

'Because she isn't in this morning, my mum said.'

'What are we going to do now?' Lauren hissed as they lined up for Assembly. 'If anything happens to Caroline . . .'

'Shut up a minute and let me think,' Alex hissed back.

'Well, you better think quick. It was your idea.'

'Oh, thanks. I don't have to do this, you know . . .'

'Fine!' Lauren flung herself away from Alex and out of the line. 'Don't do it then!'

'Oohh, what's up with them two?' Andrea sniggered to the girl behind. 'Lovers' tiff?'

'Shut up, Andrea, or I'll break your scrawny little neck.' Alex turned round and grabbed her by the collar. Andrea yowled in protest.

'What's going on back there?' Mrs Bridges shouted from the door.

Alex yanked Lauren back next to her. The other girl tried to shake her off but Alex held her wrist tightly.

'Stop being so stupid,' Alex said out of the corner of her mouth. 'I can't help it if Quaid's not here yet.'

Mrs Bridges followed them back to the classroom and settled herself at Ms Quaid's desk with a pile of marking.

'Any questions?' she inquired, after rattling through what they had to do.

'Yes,' Alex asked. 'When's Ms Quaid coming back?'

'She'll be back at lunch-time,' Mrs Bridges snapped, biting off each word and glaring at Alex. 'Not that it's got anything to do with you. I can't see that a member of staff's personal affairs are any of your business, Alex Lewis.' She turned away, addressing the class as a whole. 'I don't want to hear another word out of any of you. The work's written up on the board so you better get on with it.'

The morning stretched out. Alex had assured Lauren that Caroline would be safe, but there was a long way to go between now and lunch-time and she couldn't guarantee it. She kept her head down, pretending to work, looking up now and again. She needed to get to Lauren, work out what they should do, but it was hopeless. Mrs Bridges was like one of those lizard things that can move its eyes round in different directions. One eye remained focused on the books in front of her while the other restlessly swivelled in her head, scanning the room for the slightest movement or any sign of talking.

By break the heavy rain that started soon after nine, had slackened off. It looked like they would be able to go out after all. Alex got up slowly. She would have preferred it if the whole school had been kept in. At least Caroline would have been safe in her classroom then.

By the time they got outside the rain had stopped and the sun was trying to come out, but there were big puddles everywhere and the trees were still dripping. Lauren threw up the hood of her sweatshirt and took a bunch of papers out of the pouch at the front.

'I found all these in my desk,' she said, handing them to Alex.

Alex turned up her collar and looked down at the crumpled slips of paper. Water dripped from the eaves, smudging the crude capitals and felt-tip drawings of mis-shapened skulls and daggers dipped in blood. Some of the coffins had R.I.P. CAROLINE written on them, others LOREN R.I.P. ALEX LEWIS dripped red with a knife through it. She shoved them into the pocket of her denim jacket.

A few people were out and running around, but most of the senior school were not in any hurry to go outside. Lauren and Alex splashed through sheets of water, pacing the uneven surface of the playground in moody silence.

'What are we going to do, Alex?' Lauren asked at last. 'Do you think we ought to—'

'What?' Alex demanded. 'Go home and get the money? I haven't got that much, have you? Anyway, what can they do? Our mums are coming up this afternoon.'

Lauren glanced around. Sudden sun had brought more people into the yard. She searched the crowds for Sandi and Greg and the rest of the Bridge Boys but, to her relief, could see no sign of them.

'Yeah, I know,' she sighed, 'it's just Caroline. I get worried.'

The bell rang to signal the end of their break and the beginning of the Infants' time.

'She'll be OK,' Alex said, listening to the clamour set up by the younger pupils as they streamed out. 'She's safe in there.' She indicated the wall that separated the two playgrounds. 'Safe as houses.'

'I guess you're right,' Lauren said with a grin. 'Come on, we better go in.'

They turned away then, to go back to their class-room, so they didn't see Sandi go into the Infants' playground. Neither did the teacher on break duty because, at exactly that moment, she had to go over and sort out a scuffle that had broken out amongst a group of boys.

'It's nothing, Miss, honest,' Greg Simpson began to explain, 'just a game that's got a bit out of hand. We're only playing, Miss.'

Sandi's business didn't take long. She whistled as she went past and suddenly the boys stopped exclaiming their innocence and arguing amongst themselves. They went back to their classes happily enough and the teacher returned to her playground duty. She sipped her tea and grimaced with disgust, it was nearly cold. The quarrel had been over something and nothing as far as she could tell, but it had taken a good couple of minutes to get it sorted.

Alex and Lauren had agreed to try and act as natural as possible in the dining room at lunch-time but, as soon as she saw Greg coming over, Alex's heart started to thump. Her hand was shaking as she took out the tape recorder and placed it on the table, caged from sight.

'What do you think you're doing?'

Greg Simpson was leaning across the dinner table towards Lauren. His breath smelt of cheese and salami sandwich.

'I said, what are you doing here?'

'I'm eating my lunch like everybody else,' Lauren replied. 'What does it look like?'

'You're not supposed to' – he raised his voice so others could hear – 'because you aren't like everybody else, are you?' He put his fists on the table either side of her and said quietly, 'You know what will happen if you don't get it.'

'Get what?'

'The money. You were told – get it or else.'

'Or else what?'

'Or else your sister gets a haircut . . .'

'I really don't think you're going to do that,' Alex interrupted.

Simpson grinned, his eyes gleaming between closing lids. 'Recognize this?'

He took something out of the pocket of his baseball jacket, holding it so only they could see the grubby green-and-white spotted ribbon with the ends fraying that Caroline had been wearing that morning. His grin widened to its full wolfish extent at the look on Lauren's face as she saw that a thin tail of fair hair was still attached to it.

'Little kids can be so trusting, don't you find that, Alex?' He laughed softly, shaking his head. 'That's just for starters, so you know not to mess me about.' In the space of a breath, the mockery in his voice hardened to menace. 'Get the money or I'll do her properly, with this.' He uncurled the fingers of his other hand so they could see the wood- and brass-handled knife. 'You too. It's a promise.'

Alex's heart felt squeezed and heavy in her chest. It was difficult to breathe. They had to do something. Right now. But what? She stared up at him. She felt Lauren's arm was shaking against hers and her own mouth was dry. Fear made it hard to think.

'Would you mind repeating that, perhaps a little bit louder.' Alex moved her hands away and spoke, trying to control the tremor in her voice, directly into the recorder. 'Maybe you'd like to describe for the ladies and gentlemen that knife you've got hidden.'

'What's that?'

Simpson's grin faded. He had not expected this. An expression a little like fear came sneaking across his face.

'It's a tape recorder, what do you think it is?' Alex said quietly. Suddenly she felt very calm. 'It's got everything you've said so far. Like to add any further comment?'

Simpson didn't say anything. He made a grab, but Alex had skimmed it away from him. Dave Morris caught it and passed it to Neil Freeman.

'Go straight to Quaid,' he said, without taking his eyes off the three at the end of the table.

Neil nodded and stood up. He quickly made his way to the door, glad he could do something. Dave could not go himself. He had to stay, in case Alex and Lauren needed his help.

Greg surged to follow him but Lauren grabbed his arm.

'He's taking it.' She held onto his sleeve, twisting the material so he could not break away from her. 'And you listen. My mother and hers are coming in to see the Head this afternoon and if anything happens to us, or my sister, the police are going to be informed.'

Greg Simpson looked round for his usual support, but at the mention of the police his gang had melted back to their seats and were taking a new interest in their lunch-boxes. He turned round to find Mrs Brody, the chief dinner supervisor, glaring down at him.

'What's going on here?' she said, pushing Simpson back into his place.

'Nothing. Just having a chat, Miss.' Simpson shut his lunch-box and made to get up.

'Just a minute.' The dinner lady stood over him, arms folded.

'He's got a knife, Miss,' Dave Morris said quietly.

'Yeah, where?' Greg tried to put on his usual mask of insolence, but the fear had grown in his eyes and his voice was high and panicky. 'Any of you seen one?' He looked round. When no one said anything some of his cockiness returned. 'Go ahead and search me.'

He stood up and started emptying his pockets.

'It's in his sandwiches,' Dave said to the dinner lady. 'Look in his lunch-box.'

Her hand was on the box a second before Greg's.

'Open it!' she ordered.

He slowly peeled off the plastic top.

'See?' He grinned. 'What did I tell you? Nothing.'

'Look inside the sandwich, Mrs Brody,' Dave said.

'Get it out!' She looked down at him, arms folded. 'Hold it up, higher, where I can see.'

Greg shielded the mangled bread and butter with his hand.

'Open it up.'

'There's nothing there. Honest. Believe me. Just filling, please . . .'

He was beginning to babble now under her stony gaze. Eventually he had to do as she said. The knife was there, everyone saw it, covered in butter and salami.

'It ain't a proper blade. It's just a penknife, for Christ's sake. Anyway,' he added, 'it's too short to do any damage.'

He dropped it then, kicking it across the room towards his gang but none of them made any move to pick it up.

'What was it doing in your sandwiches then? Funny place to keep a pocket knife.' Mrs Brody ignored the ripple of sniggers and stared steadily at Simpson. 'You go and pick that – thing – up and bring it to me.'

But he was off, running for the door, sending

empty chairs flying. Trays crashed from the trolley by the entrance, spilling leftover food all over the place, and the doors swung wildly back and forth. A tray spun itself slowly to a standstill and cutlery clattered to a halt somewhere under the tables on the far side of the floor.

'Are you all right, dear?' Mrs Brody bent down over Lauren. 'He's a nasty one, he is, just like his brother. Little toe rags, the pair of them. Did you see that, Maggie?' She turned to the woman behind the hatch who was shaking her head. 'The Head's going to hear about this. It's criminal. Criminal behaviour. I'm not having that happening in my dining hall.'

Chapter 22

The Head flicked off the tape recorder. The voices and the muffled dining-hall noises of half an hour before died in the silence of his office. His mouth compressed into a thin line until you could hardly see it, as he surveyed the crude drawings on the crumpled notes scattered across the neat papers stacked on his desk.

'I've already spoken to Mrs Brody about what happened this dinner-time,' he said, 'and I'm taking it seriously, very seriously indeed. From what you've just told me' – he nodded to Ms Quaid, seated by the side of his desk, and towards Alex and Lauren, sitting in front of him on the edge of the same chair – 'it appears to be the last in a whole catalogue of things that add up to quite brutal and systematic bullying.' He pushed a hand through his curly blond hair. 'The incident earlier in the week, the letters home, Ms Quaid did express considerable concern. But, well' – he indicated the piles of paperwork in front of him – 'there are so many other things – I'm afraid I did rather dismiss it as six of one and half a dozen of the other. I shouldn't have. I'm sorry. It's my mistake and I owe you an apology.'

He smiled at them then, and reached for his pen.

'Alex, Lauren, you can go now. Ms Quaid won't be long, but there are a few things I need to talk with her about. Take this to Mrs Bridges. It explains what kept you.'

He tore the hastily scrawled note off the pad and handed it to Lauren. The two girls got up to go.

'Mr Derby,' Ms Quaid said, folding her arms, 'I think they ought to stay. It took a lot of guts to tell us what was going on and I think they are entitled to know what we're going to do about it.'

'Yes, of course. Well . . .' He pushed his chair back and stood up abruptly, towering over them. For a moment Alex thought he was angry with them and began to feel worried. He caught her look and sat down again. 'Starting with Simpson . . .'

'He's skipped,' Ms Quaid said. 'Run out of school.'

'He's also excluded. His parents can find him somewhere else to continue his education. The others are suspended as from now and they won't come back until I've seen them with their parents. I'm going to stamp this out once and for all – even if they have to stay in after school from now until the end of term.' He turned to Alex and Lauren, his tone more kindly now. 'If they try and come back at you, or anything else happens, anything at all, you must come straight to me. Promise?' The two girls nodded. 'I'm going to seek expert advice on this, look at all the aspects. We need to get a programme started.' He looked over at Alex and their eyes met. 'Things are different now. Different from the past . . .'

Alex was not sure if she was meant to reply so she stayed silent.

'Bullies need help too, you know. Don't they, Ms Quaid?' he said after a while.

'Yes,' their teacher agreed, 'maybe even more than the people they bully.'

Just then the intercom buzzed on his desk.

'Mrs Lewis and Mrs Price to see you,' the disembodied voice announced.

'Send them in please, Sally,' he said, pressing a switch down. 'And do you think you could see about getting us some coffee?'

As soon as they were out of the Head's office, Lauren was off. Alex had trouble catching up with her and only just managed to dodge the teacher on duty between the Senior and Junior playgrounds.

They found Caroline sitting in the soft play area, patiently sorting through the wood chippings. Her head was bent and Alex could see that her long fair plait was now secured by a brown elastic band. The end was a fat little stub and looked a bit like a thick-bristle paintbrush.

'Are you all right?' Lauren's question came out in gasps. She'd got there fast and was having trouble getting her breath back.

'Of course I am,' Caroline replied without even glancing up. 'Don't stand there, Lauren. I haven't checked that bit yet. You could be squashing hundreds.'

'Hundreds of what?' Alex asked.

'Hundreds of woodlice. They live in this stuff.' Caroline stirred the chippings with her right hand. 'I'm collecting them up and when I've got enough, I'm going to take 'em and put 'em down Yvonne Mitchell's knickers.'

140

'Oh, no you're not,' Lauren said quietly. 'Let them go.'

Alex flinched as Caroline reluctantly opened her grimy fist and a collection of the grey-armoured creatures scurried off.

'Now stand up,' Lauren ordered, 'and tell us exactly what happened.'

'They conned me,' Caroline muttered angrily. 'That fat Yvonne in Class Four and her sister, Sandi. They bet me fifty pence I wouldn't cut the end off my plait, and when I did, they wouldn't pay up. Then Sandi yanked my ribbon and just ran off. It's one of my favourite ones and I want it back. I reckon you're right about this crew, Lo,' she added, looking round. 'They're a real load of scrags and snots, the whole lot of them.'

Chapter 23

Seven Q was very quiet on Monday, very subdued. The class looked too small for the room with Sandi, Greg and the Bridge Boys missing.

It is strange how quickly things can change, Alex thought, as she reached in her desk for her reading book. She and Lauren had gone from virtual outcasts, with only each other for company, to almost heroes, in the space of just a few days. Alex found this difficult to handle. No one had said sorry or anything, they just chattered nervously, fussing around, and she felt smothered by all the attention.

'I'd really like you to come, Alex,' Josie was saying.

She had phoned Sunday afternoon to ask and, as soon as they were in school, had started again. She was now practically begging Alex to go to her Birthday Barbecue and Disco.

'And Lauren, too,' she was saying now. 'Will you ask her?'

Alex had wanted to refuse at first. Especially since, with Sandi out and no one speaking to Andrea, it looked a bit as though she'd was a last-minute addition to a shrinking guest list. But she talked it over with her mum and they'd both agreed, there was no point in bearing grudges.

'Yes,' she said to Josie, 'I'll come. But I can't say for Lauren. You'll have to ask her yourself.'

Josie looked suddenly uncertain, but she was going over to Lauren's table. She hovered for a moment or two, swallowed a couple of times, and then went ahead. Lauren's eyes clouded and her brows drew together. Alex was sure she was going to say no, but she didn't. She smiled and shrugged. 'Yes, why not?'

Josie came back, grinning smugly, announcing that they'd all been wrong about Lauren: she was really nice when you got to know her.

'Hey, Dave. Where are you going?' Alex shouted.

The two boys waited at the corner.

'We've got to move our bikes,' they said when the girls caught up. 'Something to do with the new classrooms.'

The bike sheds were next to the school pond at the back of the school, tucked away with the bins and everything else no one wanted to see, behind a block of decrepit terrapin huts. When they got there the whole area was swarming with men in fluorescent bibs and hard hats. Some of them were squinting along instruments and others were rolling out bits of string, measuring.

'Why have we got to move 'em, mate?' Dave called to one of the men.

'Need a clear line for the theodolite.'

Dave shook his head, puzzled.

'Measuring up,' the man explained. 'Whole lot's coming down. From here,' he indicated with his thumb, 'to over there.' He pointed to the wall past the caretaker's garage. 'And, come the end of the summer, there'll be a whole new block.'

'That's the caretaker's garage!'

'Got to come down, son. Riddled with dry rot. Anyway, it ain't really a garage and it ain't really his. It belongs to the Council.'

The man frowned, puzzled by the children's odd reaction. You'd think they'd be glad to get nice new classrooms, he thought, as he turned away to get on with his job.

The small group stood in silence, taking in what they had just been told. Bailey's garage was going. One of the school's special places was scheduled for demolition. It was a secret landmark, a place of story and legend, and after the summer it would be gone. It just wouldn't be there any more.

Dave reared up, acting their thoughts out for them, pulling terrible faces and making unearthly shrieking noises. Some of the workmen started to laugh.

'Michael Bailey, Michael Bailey,' he intoned. 'Poor restless spirit. Where will you go?'

'Shut up, Dave! Stop being stupid!' Alex shouted.

'Just a joke, Alex!' Dave called out to her, but she was already walking away.

Back in the yard, Dave and Neil joined the rest of the boys in their never-ending year-round football game, but for the girls it was the skipping season. A lot of the Year Seven girls reckoned they were too old for it now, but they could usually be persuaded. Andrea wandered around looking for people to play.

She might not be much good at anything else, but Andrea was the best skipper in the playground. She could do French skipping, Norwegian skipping, any number of fancy steps. And she had the best rope. It was proper, long and strong with firm handles, whipped against fraying, not cheap clothes-line. It dangled from her bag in fat loops like a thick blue snake but, today, it wasn't tempting anyone. Each group she approached ignored her. She turned away finally, tears spilling and her glasses misting up. She blinked rapidly and took them off, polishing them viciously on her cardigan.

'Hi, Andrea. See you've got your rope. Fancy a skip?'

She quickly replaced her glasses and squinted up at Alex Lewis.

'Are you taking the . . .'

'No.' Alex laughed. 'Honest. Come on. Get out your rope. We'll have a game. You, me, and Lauren.'

'Hey,' Lauren said. She was as taken aback as Andrea. 'Hang on a minute, Alex . . .'

Alex turned to her. 'What's the matter? I thought we agreed, bygones are bygones, remember?'

'It's, it's not that . . .' her voice dropped to an urgent whisper and she pulled Alex away from the other girl. 'I can't skip, Alex.'

'You can turn a rope, can't you? Anyway, it's easy. Andrea's an expert – she'll teach you. Won't you?'

Andrea nodded her head and started to get out her rope. She was still suspicious about what Alex was up to, but anything was better than being on her own all the time with no one to play with. She gave one end of the rope to Lauren and took the other herself. The two girls drew apart from each other.

'OK!' Alex shouted. 'Start turning.'

The rope swished round and hit the ground. Alex counted herself in.

'All in together, girls.
Never mind the weather, girls.
If you want a boyfriend please jump in . . .'

Alex's voice echoed off the playground walls and the knots and groups of girls turned to stare.

'. . . please jump in . . . please jump in.'

The repeated phrase gradually brought them over. In ones and twos at first, and then more. Josie and then Melanie joined Alex under the turning rope, and then others joined until it could hold no more.

'Spanish Lady! Spanish Lady!' someone shouted.

Andrea handed her end of the rope over to another. It was her cue. The others made way for her as she jumped in. She counted a couple of turns on the rope and then began to execute the complex shouted instructions perfectly.

'Keep the kettle boiling!' another voice shouted as Andrea left to a scatter of applause.

A ragged queue formed as the new chant started up. Andrea held out her hand for Lauren's end of the rope.

'No, I told you. I can't skip.' Lauren kept on turning.

'Come on. Give it to me,' Andrea said. 'I'll tell you what to do. It's easy.'

Lauren handed over the rope and joined the queue. She watched nervously, dreading her turn, as the girls in front dodged in and out with practised ease.

'Now,' Andrea hissed when she was next, 'start counting the turns of the rope. When you see it coming down... Now! jump in! Keep jumping! Keep jumping!'

Lauren ignored the encouraging shouts from the rest of the girls to concentrate on what her legs were doing. Once you got a rhythm going it was easy.

'Now jump out!'

Andrea's voice came to her but she was a split second too late. She misjudged the turns of the rope and it tangled round a foot. She would have gone sprawling if Josie hadn't caught her.

They were all laughing, even Alex. But their laughter was different now. Lauren found herself joining in.

'You weren't bad,' Andrea remarked, as Lauren hobbled back, rubbing her ankle, 'considering. Alex, chuck us the other end – better pack it in now – bell's going to go. But,' she looked at the two girls, her eyes magnified by the thick lenses, 'what about dinner-time? Do you fancy it?'

'Yes.' Alex nodded. 'Why not?'

When they got to the line, Andrea dodged in next to Josie and the other girls beckoned them over; but Alex and Lauren stayed slightly apart, still not sure whether to trust them or not. But, in the end, it didn't really matter. Alex returned Lauren's smile as Ms Quaid called them in. What did they need the rest of them for? They always had each other.

Chapter 24

'Lauren? Can you play tennis?'

Alex lay with her arms behind her head, staring up at the ceiling. She was staying at Lauren's house. It was the last weekend of the Whitsun holidays and, if they kept the noise down, they could lie in the darkness chatting all night if they wanted to, about anything and everything.

'Yeah, a bit,' Lauren replied. 'I used to play when we lived in Perth. But I'm not brilliant or anything.'

'You've got to be better than me. Do you think you could show me?'

'Yes, I suppose so. Why?'

'Well,' Alex squirmed about in her sleeping bag. 'Dave Morris keeps asking me to play and I don't want to keep saying "No" but I'm absolutely hopeless.'

Lauren laughed. 'Oh, I see . . .'

'No, you don't.' Alex struggled up onto her elbows. 'It's not like that!'

Lauren leaned over the side of the bed, grinning wickedly. 'Isn't it?'

'No, we're just friends . . .'

'Don't worry, Alex, your secret's safe with me. Anyway, he's really nice – and cute looking.'

'I keep telling you . . .'

'OK, OK. We could go down the park tomorrow. You can borrow Mum's racquet.'

'Right.' Alex settled back. 'Let's do that. But don't tease me about it.'

Lauren laughed. 'OK, I promise.'

They were quiet for so long Alex thought Lauren was asleep. She lay looking up at the masks on the wall. They should have been even more frightening in the shadowed half-light, filtering in from the street outside, but they were not; they looked mysterious and powerful. Lauren had told her that they made them hideous to scare off evil spirits. Maybe there was something in that, Alex thought to herself.

'You never told me exactly what happened to him.'

Lauren's voice in the dark was unexpected. It startled Alex.

'Happened to who?' she asked.

'Michael Bailey. What happened to Michael Bailey?'

'What made you think about him?'

'I don't know.' Lauren yawned. 'I was thinking about going to the park that day when Caroline disappeared and how we both ended up at Bailey's garage.'

'That's strange,' Alex said. 'I was thinking about him too – kind of. I saw him the other day. In real life. Really.'

'When? You didn't tell me.'

'It was when you were in Scotland.'

Lauren had only just got back from a few days' holiday. Her mother, desperate to visit places she had heard about all her life but never seen, had made her husband take some time off so they could all go together as a family. Lauren had not said much, apart from she'd enjoyed the trip, but she seemed a lot happier since they got back.

'So? Tell me about it,' Lauren demanded, wide awake now. 'Tell me about meeting Bailey.'

'I'd just been into town with Mum in the car and, on the way back, she said something about going to Jean's house to pick something up. Did I tell you about Jean?'

'No.' Lauren considered for a moment. 'I don't think so. Who is she?'

'She's a woman my mum works with and she lives next door to where the Baileys live. Used to live,' Alex corrected herself. 'That's how I knew for definite he hadn't died or anything.'

'Why did everybody else think so, then? Why did they make up all those stories about him being a ghost?'

'Because he never came back, I suppose. After it happened – you know, that on the bridge, no one from school ever saw him again. He didn't even come out of his room for months, Jean said. He had some sort of breakdown. Jean talked about it to my mum, you know how they do, kind of quiet and serious when they think you aren't listening. His mum taught him at home for a while and then they moved to Milton Keynes or somewhere. That's where they live now, anyway.'

'So? What happened?'

'When we got there, to Jean's house, she said, "Hello, Alex. There's a friend of yours here. He's in the garden." I didn't have a clue who she could mean, so I went out to see. They've got sliding doors from the living room and then there's a little patio, and there he was, sitting on a white plastic chair, drinking a Pepsi.'

'What did he look like?'

'Taller, thinner, especially his face, much more grown-up looking. And his clothes were different. He was wearing jeans, and a T-shirt and trainers – like anybody else. His hair is the same, though, bright red, and falling in bars down his forehead. That's how I recognized him.'

That and the old look of wariness he gave when he recognized me, Alex thought. But she didn't want to tell Lauren about that, or the surge of shame she felt, knowing she had caused him to react like that.

'What did you talk about?'

'Things, you know. His new school, mainly. They go to secondary a year earlier than us and he really likes it. It's not too big and they've got all kinds of computers and science labs and stuff and he's really into that.'

'Did he say anything about, you know . . .'

'No. I thought he was going to . . .'

There had been a moment, when the grown-ups had gone to the kitchen to refill their glasses and catch up with the gossip, when she thought he was going to say something. They had both started speaking, and then stopped, together. He was looking straight at her. As she looked into his eyes, noticing again that strange bruised purple colour, the tranquil suburban summer afternoon faded. The bird song and the wasp buzz of a distant lawnmower changed into the rhythmic bitter sound of children's voices chanting, and they were both back on that bridge.

She had wanted to say she understood now, to apologize, to try to explain, to get rid of some of the guilt and shame. Try, however late it was, to repair some of the damage that had been done to him. But the moment passed.

'Neither of us said a word in the end,' she concluded. 'Just started talking about something else.'

'Safer that way,' Lauren said eventually. 'Maybe it's best forgotten.'

'Yes, maybe,' Alex agreed.

Lauren murmured goodnight and turned into sleep, but Alex, eyes open, stared into the darkness. Somewhere a distant church clock was striking. Alex tried not to count. Twelve. Midnight. Time the ghosts come out.

She would not forget. Neither would he. Neither would any of the people who had played the Game with Michael Bailey.